LIARS INVOLVED

A. Brenee

Dedication:

I dedicate this book to my mother, for never letting me give up on anything, and for pushing me to always do my best. To my sister Caty, who demanded that she be personally recognized, thank you for always reminding me that I have a strong literary voice. To all of my siblings, the rest of my immediate family, and all of the close friends who believed in my dream; Thank you for supporting me in this process. Finally I dedicate this book to Nairn. You are my world, my strength, and the very air that I breathe. None of this would have happened, if not for you.

Contents:

I.	Love Me as I Am	5
II.	Broken Glass and Shattered Pieces	12
III.	Heal Me, Feel Me, Sex Me	17
IV.	Fuel the Fire	23
V.	Sometimes Tomorrow isn't a Brighter Day	28
VI.	Decisions Will be Made	36
VII.	Considering Options	44
VIII.	Secrets from Our Past	53
IX.	Winning in Love	59
X.	Not What I Expected	65
XI.	Liars and Losers	71
XII.	Truth comes in Phases	80
XIII.	Revelations	91

Chapter 1
Love me as I am

It wasn't love at first sight, it was more like contentment that you were there. It wasn't that I couldn't live without you, it was the loneliness that I couldn't bear. It wasn't that you were my everything, it was more like I tolerated you being around. It wasn't that you were my true love, it was more like, I liked you, and my true love hadn't been found.

Dev

"Next time I see you, just know, that ass is mine!" I said as she turned and walked out of the room.

Luna

"Wine and Food! My two favorite words YASSS!" Tiana waved her arms above her head as she yelled across the kitchen while pouring herself a very tall glass of Mascato. Tonight was one of our regularly scheduled girls night out, which we usually planned for every other Friday; well that was the plan before I started seeing Dev. It was always me, my girls Tiana and Monique, my cousin Apryl, and my best friend Alton. The venue changes every week, from us going to lounges, or sushi bars, to just hanging out somebody's house putting on a few extra pounds. There was nothing better than catching up with friends, over fatty foods and drinks. My girls and I were down for anything as long as we could have a kee kee moment to break up the monotony of our regular lives. There wasn't much to do in Bridgeton, which is your average mediocre Midwest American town. So as a single professional woman, all I wanted to do was live my life, make good money, and meet the man of my dreams. Recently I found myself in the process of meeting my forever man, so I had missed the last three outings, messing around with Dev. What can I say, I was trying to be a loyal and devoted girlfriend. Hell, after going out on a few good dates with him, I had turned my back on my girls so fast, they had forgotten what my face looked like. Dev and I were building our relationship; so I was either at his house every night, he was at mine, or I was at some event by his side as his beautiful, yet silent girlfriend. I didn't always like being his silent partner, but he always said that he wanted to be a leader in our relationship, so sometimes I needed to be seen and not heard. I didn't always agree, but I let him have his way sometimes, just to keep the peace. Now, as I'm standing in a corner of the kitchen, everyone is laughing and joking, all reminiscing on inside jokes from their last meet up that I missed, I begin to feel left out. I dismiss the thought, since that's the risk you take when you are falling in love, or building a relationship outside of your friends. Then I smile to myself, enjoying the feelings of being in the moment. Completely embracing how happy I was to be back with my friends again.

"Lu? Where is the salsa?" Alton asked me as he's standing way too close to my face, which abruptly snaps me back into reality. Without responding, I push past him and through the herd of my greedy friends, whom were all crowded around my kitchen, to get to the fridge where the salsa was sitting plain as day in the middle of the top rack. "Ohh this salsa, that makes sense being in the fridge, and makes more sense for someone to look there?" I say sarcastically as I held the salsa in my hand and extended it in his direction. He rolled his eyes as he snatched the jar from me. We both laughed for a second, then he walks away. It wasn't unusual for Alton and I to talk on the phone every single day. But since I started dating Dev, our conversations became far and few between. I was looking for love, and for now I had someone in my life that I felt brought me one step closer to getting a ring. While I wouldn't call what Dev and I had quite "being in love" yet. I will say that I am happy that he is a decent, educated, financially stable guy. I mean let's be real, no man is perfect, they all have their flaws. I mean yeah, Dev may go out most weekends with his boys; but he always comes in before five in the morning to be with me. Even though it's usually to wake me up for sex. Don't we all want that? Then there was that one time he came in really drunk, and told me about some girl who had given him a lap dance at the club, then she casually slid her number in his pocket. I cringed at the thought. Although, he did give me the number, and told me that he would never call her because he was falling in love with me. Anyways, so I guess he isn't perfect, but he works for me. I just have to understand that he's a young man, and one day he will eventually grow up. As for now, he isn't as bad as some other losers I've dated.

The noise began to die down as everyone started to stuff their faces full of food. I noticed that there was a weird tension in the room, but why, I didn't know. Finally Apryl just came out and said the one thing that was clearly on everyone's mind. "So you're able to kick it with your girls tonight cause you're boyfriend is where again?" Sarcasm and shade spilling from her lips. "You know what, let's all get it out ladies. I've been a bad friend since I started kicking it with Dev; but y'all know how it is. When it comes to your man, and your friends, your man has to come first sometimes." I said dismissing her comment. Alton joined in as he pours an unusually large amount of salsa on top of his plate of chips. "Yeah, we know that whenever you start getting some regular D, you forget you have friends. You've done it before with plenty other boyfriends, this ain't new Luna." Monique and Tiana both shake their heads in agreement. I continue to defend myself. "You're Right! I've been preoccupied. Dev and I are trying to really develop something long term, and it's special. We both have good intentions for one another, and when you're in love it's a building process, and not to mention…." Then Tiana cuts me off. "Yeah you're building a relationship, and he's building a good situation for himself. That's why he's not your friend on social media, hardly claims you in public, nor is he ever with you most Saturday nights. Speaking of which, isn't he in Atlantic City this weekend? So that's why you're free right?" Everyone's mouth fell open for a second, as I rolled my eyes hard in her direction. We all knew she was right. Still I turned away, not wanting them to see the utter embarrassment all over my face. The room fell silent for a second, then we all grabbed our plates, glasses of wine, and walked into the living room to sit and listen to the music. I could feel their critical eyes burning a hole in the back of my head as we settled down. Finally the silence was broken when Monique asked the million dollar question. "Keep it one hundred Luna. Dev is okay, but is he really the man you see yourself with in the future?" I sat there not exactly sure how to answer them confidently. Then she continued. "You know you can do better. He's acting like he wants the freedom of being a single man, but the luxury of getting regular ass. Then here you are, being his regular piece of obedient pussy, week after week. Be honest, has he even checked in with you since he left for the weekend?" Monique fired off in a way she hasn't done to me in the past. Everyone's face scrunched up as Monique, the strong silent one, stared at me expecting that I give her a truthful answer. Even though they were all right, they didn't have to speak to me like that in front of everyone. I was hurt, mostly because I felt embarrassed for being in a relationship that from the outside looking in, was very one sided. "I know Dev has his flaws, but he always says the things I want to hear. He's supportive in ways you all don't see. No to mention I like having him around, sometimes. While you all are sitting here judging me, I am lucky to be with a guy who has as much potential as he does. All I have to do now, is get his actions to match up with the future Dev I see." That was the best answer I could come up with to get them off my back. Everyone stared at my puzzled, then they sat back, sipped their wine, and no one said a word. Tonight wasn't starting off to be the girls night I had planned for, but it's probably going to be the girls night that I needed.

Dev

The music in the club was so loud that I could barely hear the person standing next to me. "BRUH… Look at cutie over there? She's been checking you out for the last two songs dog." I look up from my drink, and turned in the direction that Sherrod was nodding. A tall thin beautiful woman with light brown skin, long hair that was obviously a weave, and huge breast that were practically climbing out of her low cut top, was standing across the bar grinning in my direction. I lick my lips and smile at her. I gesture with my free hand for her to come over. I look back at Sherrod and point as her and her friends were making their way over to us. "You know what, I may be a little buzzed, but I ain't stupid. I'm not about to let this one slip through my fingers." I slap Sherrod's hand and offer a sly smile. The young lady strolls over with her friends, and they introduce themselves as Leanna, Crystal and Janice. Leanna, the one who was checking me out, was sexy as hell from afar, but up close, she wasn't as cute as I thought. Don't get me wrong, she was pretty enough, but her body was really amazing. Naturally thin but curvy, and with huge breast that look like two melons ripe for the picking. As a breast man, she had all the curves I needed to get any job done. I lean in to whisper in her ear. "If you were my girl, I wouldn't have let you out of the house looking like this tonight. I'm sure I would've kept you busy." She smiles and giggles like a school girl, which let me know she's feeling me. Sherrod was already pulling his, I'm too cool for these hoes act, which even though I know he was attracted to them, it's just this game he likes to play to get girls to do all the work to get to know him. I don't know how he does it, acting so nonchalant all the time, but somehow he always ends up getting what he wants in the end. I slide my hand down Leanna's back, and rest my palm just above the curve of her waist, then squeeze her hip gently. "So what are you ladies drinking tonight? My boy and I got you." "We're drinking apple martini's." Leanna responded waving her hand in a circle as if she was speaking for the entire group of ladies. I wave over to the bartender to order another round, and pulled her closer into me as if she was mine. The drinks came fast, and everyone stood together talking as best we could over the loud hip hop music, which was filling the club. I wanted to get away from the

9

group, and get closer to Leanna while I still had a chance. "You wanna go dance real quick?" I ask her as she took a sip of her drink. She shook her head no to the beat of the song. "Nah, but can we go somewhere more private and talk?" She responds. I shake my head and smile in complete agreement. "Definitely!" I looked over to make sure Sherrod was straight; but by the looks of things he had Crystal fully invested into his tough guy routine. So I wave him off as we slipped away.

The further we got away from the main floor, the more muffled the music became. She held my hand gently as we walked past a few private VIP sections, which were roped off and filled with men and women drinking expensive bottles of vodka and tequila. Then out of what seemed like nowhere, we turn down a dark hallway, and around a corner, that looked like we were heading to the bathroom, but instead we ended up in a small secluded area that was tucked way in the back of the club. "How did you know this was here?" I asked Leanna, slightly intrigue that she was able to find this spot so quick and easily. "I used to work here a few years ago. I would come back here to get away from the bar for a few minutes. No one ever comes back here, so we good. Don't worry not all east coast girls are trying to stick people up." She made a gun gesture with her hand, and we both laughed. "So where you from?" She asked in her strong East Coast accent, that I was able to clearly hear now that we didn't have to scream over the music. "I'm from the Midwest. You know like cows and corn field country. Trust me, you couldn't find Bridgeton on a map if I paid you. I'm only here for the weekend, like a boys trip type deal, just to get away from our regular life shit." I looked around the dimly lit room, trying to get a feel for my surroundings. I grab her waist and pulled her closer to me. "So what else did you want to talk about?" I asked, then rubbed the back of my hand against her cheek. She smirked and reached down to rub her hand across my crotch. "We ain't really gotta talk. When I saw you tonight, I thought to myself, damn he looks good. I figured I would shoot my shot, see if you liked me too. But since you're only here for a few nights, let's just enjoy our few minutes together. I won't bite. Unless you want me to." She said, then slipped my pants open so fast that I wasn't able to stop her. She bit her lip, reached inside and grabbed me aggressively. I unconsciously let out a gasp. She giggled softly as she slowly went down on me. "This feels so good. Damn girl!" I let her go on for a few minutes, before thinking about my relationship with Luna, then I grabbed her face to stop what was happening. "Wait, wait, just stop for a second. I'm kinda in a situation back home. I can't.." She stopped me mid sentence before I could finish what I was saying. "If you really didn't want to do this, you wouldn't be here with me right now. So forget your girl tonight, and tomorrow you can be a loyal man again." She smiled, then took all of me in. "OHHH SHIT!" I let out. She had a point. What Luna don't know won't hurt her, and tonight I'm drunk, so I'm not really responsible for any of this. As my mind begins to slip away into ecstasy, I started thinking about how Luna has been stressing me out a lot lately, and this is just the thing I needed to release some… Stress.

- Lie to me, because you love me. Or love me enough, not to lie to me. —

Chapter 2
Broken glass & Shattered pieces

It comes and goes like the seasons. Love was once real, for many real reasons. Sometimes we grow up and see things for what they really are. Sometimes we never grow up, and ruin good people by taking lies way too far.

Dev & Luna

It had been two whole days since Dev had gotten back from his boys trip, and he still hadn't called me. Whenever I sent him a text, his responses were one and two word answers. He hadn't done this before, but I merely chalked it up to him not being a very talkative person. He claimed that sometimes he just wanted to unwind and not engage in deep conversations with me or anyone else, so I didn't take it personal. But somehow, this all felt a little different. He hadn't even come by to bother me for sex. Something isn't right I thought. I wanted an answer. Where was my man, and what happened while he was away? Even though I had to work in the morning, I was willing to risk going to bed late, just to be able to clear the air with my boyfriend. I jumped in the car and drove across town to his condo, to find out what was really going on.

As I'm walking up to his front door, I hear loud music, and what sounds like a party. "What the hell? Who the hell has a party on a Wednesday night." I say out loud as I begin to knock on the door. To my surprise some nasty looking chick in a black catsuit opens the door with a smile, and proceeds to ask me if I was delivering the wings. "Umm no bitch, I'm looking for Devlyn. My boyfriend, he lives here." I said aggressively pushing past her to get into the house. "DEV, where are you?"

"Aw shit, here we go. What is she doing here?" Without any control, my internal thoughts spill out of my mouth like word vomit as I get up from the couch where I was in the middle of a game with my friend Lamont. "Bruh, pause it real quick. I'll be right back." I walk through the house in the

12

direction of her big ass mouth. We meet halfway between the living room and the my kitchen. I stop her in her tracks, turn her around, and without any words I escort her up the stairs to my room. "Hey babe, what's going on? Why did you come over here without calling me?" I ask her softly, but really wanting to know why I was seeing Luna in my house, at the same time that my friends were over chilling. "Calling? Are you shitting me? I've never had to call you to come over for the last few months, so why would I call you now? Are you fucking serious?" She was clearly livid. Little did she know, I wasn't in the mood for her attitude, or for one of her strong feminist lectures today. So in order to cut all of this shit short, I had to just come out and tell her the truth. It was over, and we weren't going to fix this. Without responding to her, I turned around to reach inside my closet, grabbed a big bag that I put all of her things in, and started to hand it to her. The look on her face when she saw the bag was heart breaking, and she immediately went silent. I blow air out of my mouth, rubbed my face, then shook my head in embarrassment. I handed her a note, hugged her, then grabbed her hand as we walked out of my room, through the house in silence, and outside so we could talk in private.

I sighed again before I started to explain. "Luna I think I loved you at some point, but I don't love you anymore. I think you need to find someone who is able to love you like, YOU need. I just can't be anything more to you, and I feel like I'm wasting both of our time." Dev said with a straight calm face. I stood there silent for a little while, just trying to figure out what the FUCK he meant. How do people determine that they don't love someone anymore. Love isn't like a quarter bag of chips, you don't start full, and once you get to a point stop and throw it out. Love should be like the middle of the ocean, one should never reach the bottom. But he was standing here in front of me with the saddest look on his face, saying that he reached his bottom of love for me like the base of the shallow end of the pool. While we had recently gone through our problems, I felt like they were things we could totally work through. Nope, he was walking away from everything we were supposed to be building, because hard work in a relationship wasn't something he was willing to do. "Fine Dev, I'm out then." I grabbed the bag and looked around to see what was exactly in it. After a second or two, I reached in and pulled out a few

13

pictures of us together. I guess he tried to give them to me as some type of sick memento. I stretched out my arm to hand them back to him, but he pushed them away saying he didn't want them. "Well I don't want this shit either." I dropped them on the ground, turned and walked away. I went home thinking about the breakup the entire way. I didn't cry, or have any real physical emotion, I was just in shock. I thought, what could I have done differently? Where did things go so wrong? As I pulled into the lot of my townhouse, I had this strange sense of relief. I realized that I would no longer have to be caught up in some loveless relationship. It didn't make the breakup hurt any less, it just was a relief. But this was just day 1.

Luna

"It could all be so simple…" Saturday nights never felt so somber. The music was clear as day, but through the mental anguish I was feeling, it sounded as if I was floating under water. Nonetheless, I was laying here listening as the music continued to fill my room. The passion and pain behind Lauryn Hill's voice was everything I was feeling in my heart right now. As she belted out in my dimly lit bedroom, I laid across my bed wondering why was I so damn depressed. I started tearing up, breaking down, thinking to myself, why am I such a screw up when it comes to love? "Why does it have to be so hard to find someone who is, honest? Why haven't I found my best friend, my partner, my homie, my lover, protector? WHY?" I screamed at the top of my lungs. How have I complicated something that as Lauryn Hill put it, is so easy? Here I was trying to figure out the complexities of my situation, as if it were rocket science.

Here I am lifeless, hopeless, sprawled across my bed, with only my side table lamp illuminating my large bedroom. Tears still swelling up in my eyes as one song began fading out, then Toni Braxton started taking over. I hear her pleading for someone please come unbreak her heart. "Girl… Who is you telling?" I say out loud as if I was expecting her to respond. It wasn't like I was bitter over breaking up with him, it was more like I was upset that I was broken up again. Alone, unwanted, unloved, un…everything. I was just undone, because once again someone told me I wasn't enough for them. I reached over to look at my phone wondering who exactly I could call to fill this void; whether it was emotionally being filled, or at this point physically would be enough. I scroll through my contacts looking at all the men who would love to over and lay with me to take me to ecstasy, or at least in my opinion give me a mediocre orgasm. While men would like to believe that all women look for an emotional connection in sex; sometimes the physical is all we need to make it one more day out here. That's when I land on a familiar name, and the corners of my mouth begin to curl upward with a curious grin. "Terri… Hmm let me see what he's up to." I click on his name with my index finger, put the warm device up to my ear and wait to hear his deep voice bellowing through the earpiece. After a few rings, he picks up and eagerly greets me. "What's up Luna, how you doing?" I sigh a breath of relief knowing that he was available, and sounded at least semi eager to hear from me. "I'm good hun, how are you doing?" He goes on about how he was just laying around the house, wasting time cause he didn't feel like going out with his friends tonight. "Well why not come waste time with me? I could use some company tonight T." I say in coy, innocent, sultry voice. "What happened to your boyfriend? Remember you stopped talking to me months ago because of him? I don't want no problems Lulu, if you have a man, I don't feel comfortable coming over and he has a key to your spot." Annoyed that he would even bring that up, I think to say, do you wanna hit this or not? Instead I sigh as if I'm exhausted. "Dev and I… we broke up, he said he doesn't love me the way I need to be loved. I'm just looking for a friend tonight; or in your case, maybe more than that. Honestly I'm really feeling down, and I'm not trying to cry on your shoulder, I just want you to hold me, cuddle with me, just lay with me and watch a movie ya know?" Now that I got his attention, I could hear him shuffling around his house looking for something. "Damn Lu.. I didn't expect to hear that. I'm really sorry to hear that this happened to you. Dude was lame anyway, I tried to tell you that the first time I saw y'all out together. But I got you, I'll come through in a few minutes. You want me to bring you anything? You want me to get some food or something drink?" I had him in my grasp now, I thought to myself. I continued to lay there listening to him talk, but then took a good look at my horrible appearance from the top down, and I knew I needed to stall him for a little while so that I could get my life together. "You know what, I could use some snacks, and something to drink. So take your time, get a couple things, whatever you bring is cool, just come by in about let's say thirty minutes. I'll be waiting for you." I smirk a little harder as we hung up the phone. Even if he isn't my man, and this may not ever be real love; I'd at least let it feel real for a moment in time.

Since he only lived about fifteen minutes away, and the whole liquor and food stop would give me an extra ten to fifteen minutes, I had to hurry up and get into my sexy girl swag. I stood up from the bed to take full inventory of my current appearance in my full body mirror, and truth is I look like a bum. No I mean really like a bum. Two different scarves, dirty sweat pants with holes in all the wrong places, an old tee shirt, that I think used to be red but is somehow now a strange shade of pink and orange. "Oh my god. Is this crust in the corner of my mouth?" I say as I wipe it away, then notice how dry my lips are due to the lack of moisture. I run to the bathroom to begin the necessary process of getting my life all the way together.

Amazingly, it only took me about twenty minutes to get my snatch back. Freshly showered, covered myself with raw cocoa butter, slid into a sexy purple nighty, and sprayed on some perfume, perfectly named Delicious. I was ready to be the main course on the menu for a night full of pleasure. Just as I was shoving some clothes from my bedroom floor into the closet, I heard a tap on my door. "Damn that was quick!" I said out loud, then screamed down the stairs that I'll be there in a second. I took one last look at myself in my mirror, reminded the woman I saw before me that she is beautiful, pushed one of my renegade curls behind my ear, and plastered a "I'm so happy to see you" smile on my face. I rushed down my stairs, strolled over to the front door, butterflies fluttering in my stomach from knowing that just on the other side was someone who was willing, and able, to have me more focused on feeling better. I swung opened the door expecting to see a tall six foot four chocolate god. Shocked and appalled, my smile quickly faded, because the person standing in front of me was not Terri, but rather...... "Gerald?"

- Surprises can be good or bad. I only like the good ones. –

16

Chapter 3

Heal me, Feel me, Sex me

Do you miss me when I'm gone? Do you reach out for me like a ghost haunting your daydreams? Do you think about the memories we once shared like precious yesterdays, and long for our tomorrows, like the hopes of what will never come? Do you miss me, now that I'm gone? Can you feel me breathing on your neck, like a lovers breath in the middle of the night? Can you taste my flesh, warm and inviting as you place your mouth on your new lovers lips? Wanting so desperately to open your eyes and see mine, but instead you find that she will never be anything like me. Do you miss me now? Will you ever?

Luna

"Gerald? What are you doing here?" I asked surprised to see him standing at my front door unannounced. So, Gerald obviously isn't my ex-boyfriend, he wasn't even the ex before that. He was like my ex four times removed. We dated the year I left undergrad, and started this long tumultuous relationship that went on and off for about two and a half years. When we finally called it quits, he and I agreed, after some time of course, that we would always remain just friends. The reality is we are much better friends, than we were anything else. You see, Gerald was, and is, a serial non-committer. He is the type of guy that wants his women to be completely committed to him, and he will only be semi committed. You know, he's the guy who's committed to you when you're around, but single everywhere else. He used to go around telling everyone that he's keeping his options open, but would tell me how much he loves everything about me, and how he couldn't wait to spend the rest of his life with me. Yeah right. Now, at thirty-five years old, Gerald is a senior account manager for a major financial company about an hour north of me. So why he was here in my town tonight; I had no idea. He has plenty of female prospects in his city, yet he still finds his way into my direct messages every few months asking me if I'm single. Yet and still, none of that had anything to do with why he was knocking on my door tonight. I knew Terri would be here any second, so this was not the night for him to be showing up trying to rekindle some dead ass flame we had years ago.

As I stood there in the doorway half-naked, still in shock and horror seeing him in front of me, I quickly tried to turn around to grab anything to cover myself up. The warm outside air began pouring into my cool living room, as I picked up the throw blanket from my sofa, using it as a cover for my body. It was evident that we both weren't expecting to see one another like this, which made us both turn our heads slightly to one side, as if we were wondering which one would be the first to speak. I wasted no time since Terri was on his way, and I needed this genius gone ASAP. "Hi Gerald! Sweetie…" I say through clinched teeth, clap both hands together, sigh aloud with a condescending grin and matching tone. "So Gerald babe. WHY ARE YOU HERE? I mean really? WHY ARE YOU AT MY DOOR AT THIS TIME OF NIGHT UNANNOUNCED?" He stood there apparently shocked at the fact that I wasn't interested in seeing him, and yet he was intrigued with what I was wearing. His five foot eleven, two hundred ten pound average frame, stood in my door with a single rose, half grinning, and half nervous to start speaking. I was neither happy, nor surprised in a good way to see him. He was fidgeting with his shirt, but he composed himself slightly, and began to speak as if he had been practicing his lines the entire fifty minute drive over. "Luna, I saw on your page this week that you broke up with your boyfriend, and figured that this would be the best opportunity for us to really start over again, and give t…." "NO. Just, NO." Before he could even finish his statement, I had to cut his crazy ass off. "Gerald, let me say this. Tonight is not the night for this, I have friends coming over soon, and we are going to have a pajama party. I wasn't expecting you, so seeing you here now, this is a bit much. Next time, you need to call before you come. And second, even if we were going to start over, this is not the correct way to do things G. Come On… Go home, I'll call you later." He could tell I was rushing to get him to go away; but I had to be short and abrupt so that he got the message that I was trying to convey. You ain't the one tonight playa; So kick rocks! Gerald lowered his head like a sad puppy, and huffed and puffed as he began to walk off. As he turned to

18

walk away, I started to feel bad about how I spoke to him, so I told him to wait for me to put on my slippers and a jacket so that I can walk him to his car. I also wanted to check to see if Terri was here, so it was a really more about me then about making him feel better. He turned and huffed again. "Naw you good Luna, I get it." In the saddest voice I had ever heard. Why he sounded like he just got the news that someone ran over his cat and there was no saving it, I will never know. Either way, I still needed to see if Terri was outside, so I yelled at him again to hold on. "Gerald, I said wait, I'm going to walk with you." I rushed to grab my jacket that was hanging in my living room closet, slid into some slipper sandals that were sitting close by, and rushed out the door, leaving it slightly cracked in case it was locked and I didn't have my keys. I caught up to him barely halfway down the path in front of my townhouse, then realized just how good it felt outside. Under normal circumstances, given I wasn't naked under the jacket, I would have been able to walk out in just some shorts and a tee-shirt. I grabbed his free hand that wasn't holding the rose, and looked up into his dark brown eyes, and mouth I'm Sorry. Softly I begin to tell him how sorry I was for being so rude before. "Gerald, you are someone I really care about, always have and always will. However, this breakup with Dev is still new for me, and I haven't even figured out how to feel about things yet. I guess I just need some time to process this whole thing, and tonight I didn't plan on processing this situation with you popping up at my crib like some Sneaky Mc. Creeper. How about when you get home, after you get some rest, I will call you tomorrow? That way, we can formally catch up over lunch or coffee. What do you say?" We arrived at his car as I finished, and I grab the rose from his hand so that he could open his door. He smiled a little, climbed inside and rolls down the window. I cross my arms and gently lean in on his driver's side window, I chew on my lower lip like an innocent little angel, knowing in the back of my mind that I had some sinning coming my way shortly. But if he doesn't get out of my parking lot real soon, I won't be getting anything. He shook his head reluctantly and said, "Yeah Lu, I feel you. I just talked to your friend Ashley yesterday, and she told me about your breakup, so I knew that this could be our last chance to try to work things out. You're right I should have called, but I wanted to come by as a surprise and comfort you. I figured you must have been pretty lonely. So that's why I popped up. You will call me in the morning, promise? We can get some breakfast or something. On me." He smirked with hope in his eyes, and I shook my head in agreement. I leaned over to kiss his cheek, knowing that he felt some sense of hope, but the truth is I was only giving him a false sense of reality. I didn't EVER want be with Gerald again, because he wasn't ever going to change his ways. So I let him have his hope for tonight, said my goodbyes, and rushed him off. "Thank you for understanding love, I'll talk to you tomorrow babe." I turned around quickly as I heard a noise behind me as Gerald drove away. I saw a shadowy figure headed right for my door, coming from the opposite side of my building. "Please God, let that be Terri." I say as I squint my eyes trying to focus on who it was this time. "YES!" I say thankfully. I was so glad that there were two different ways to park near my townhouse. One was through the front gate, which is the way Gerald took, and the second was the back gate, which Terri had come through, by the grace of the universe. I quickly shuffled up the walk towards the door seeing his arms filled with goodies as we made eye contact. His beautiful chocolate lips opened up to a pearly white smile that just melted me like butter in a hot pan. I mean great googly moogly, Terri is FINE! "Hey baby girl, who was that you were just talking to?" He asked in his sexy deep voice. Before I answered him, reached out to grab the back of his neck and pulled him into a hug that I intended to last a minute too long. I breathed him in deeply, and let out a sigh of relief as I let go of him and stepped back into the light to catch my balance. I dismiss the idea that I was speaking to anyone important. "Ohh that, it was nothing. Just was a friend who owed me some money, and came to bring it back. No biggie." I look him up and down taking in how wonderful he looked. Dressed in light grey sweat pants, a white tee-shirt with the deep v neck, and black sneakers, he looked magically delicious. If I saw him out in public, I would definitely flirt my ass off if I didn't know him. "I'm so glad you came by." I blush and giggle, as I'm trying to subconsciously send him my *I wanna hump you* vibes. I grab his hand, toss the rose Gerald gave me into the bushes, and lead Terri into my house. I'm twisting my hips ever so slightly, well maybe a bit more than usual, giving him a full blown show as I lead him into the kitchen. He sets his bags on the counter, and begins to pull fruit, honey, whipped cream, and Champagne out.

Just as I think he's done, he pulls out a long slender bottle of vodka, which I think he brought over for us to take shots. Instead, he begins to search for a bowl in my kitchen. "Why do you need a bowl for the vodka?" I ask confused. "I'm gonna teach you something new today. I'm going to soak some of the fruit in it. Trust me, you'll love it." He says and smiles in my direction, as he's looking up from the cabinet on the floor next to my stove. I smirk and think to myself, vodka soaked fruit seems like the type of adventure I need in my life right now.

We stood around the kitchen chit chatting as he continued to prep for a some time. I still had my jacket on, but was ready to take it off any minute. He walked past me towards the living room then turned back around to ask me a question. "Can I use one of those blankets on the couch?" He asked picking up the one I previously used as a body shield with Gerald. I agreed. He could have asked me to stand on my head and recite the pledge of allegiance in that moment, and as fine as he is, I would have said yes to that too. I followed behind him after a second, and watched as he started to set up a make shift picnic on my living room floor. He walked back to the kitchen and emerged carrying what I thought was everything he brought. I was overly impressed at his ability to carry what seemed like all the things he prepared in one trip to the living room. I ran back and grabbed the bowl of vodka drenched strawberries and pineapples, two wine glasses, and a fork I kept gripped between my front teeth, and I struggled the whole way. We finally sat down, and I ask in a shy sexy tone, "So what should I try first?" I gently bend my head down and look up at him through the corner of my eyes, letting him know I'm only teasing. Secretly, the frisky side of me just wants him to tell me what to do. He never looked in my direction, as he was obviously more focused on pouring champagne in the glasses, then he was on me trying to be cute. Since it was clear that he wasn't picking up what I was putting down, I said it again. "What should I try first T?" He responds dryly "Lulu, don't play with me, eat whatever you want." Now I'm a bit disappointed, until I he says, "But if you want me to feed you, I can play that game too." "Ohh you can, huh?" I said as he smirked then took a huge strawberry which seemed to have doubled in size from soaking in the alcohol. He dipped it into some honey and went to slide it into my mouth. As he leaned in to feed me, he brushed the fruit slightly against my chin. "Oops, looks like I got you a little bit. Now what should I do about that Luna?" He said in the sexiest joking voice I had heard in a long time. I shook my head as if I didn't know, then he leaned in and gently kissed me, then used his soft tongue to remove the left over honey from my face. My body trembled as he proceeded to softly kiss my neck. I moaned, then without warning I pulled away. I heard something outside my living room window, that I was hoping not to hear. I don't think Terri heard the same awful sound, because he kept trying to get my attention back onto him. "Now that's rude. I'm helping you out, and this is how you repay me? Come over here and kiss me Luna!" He demanded as he continued to pull me back into him, but I put both my hands into his chest and pushed him away. "Okay, did I do something wrong?" He asked as I jumped up. I shook my head, but continued to walk towards my door. Hoping that the sound outside my house was only a figment of my imagination, or that somehow I'm either dreaming, or slightly losing my mind. But there it is again, "Luuuuuuuuu.. LUUUUNNNNAAAA! Luna, Luna, Luna, Luna, LuuuNAAHHH!" I drop my head down in embarrassment, and whimper gently "ohh no, no, no, no, no, no." I turn around ask Terri to give me one second while I tend to the drama outside. I get up, grab my jacket once again, open the door only to see my very drunk, very loud cousin Apryl with my most recent ex boyfriend in tow. "Sweet Lawd this can't be my life!"...

- Why must we play these games? I told you I don't understand these rules. -

Chapter 4

Fuel the fire

"In my Solitude, you stood just far enough away to watch me in my pain. Shame and grief surrounded me, but you never came to my rescue. Drowning, sinking, wailing inside of the crashing waves; trying to stay afloat, but quickly headed towards my early grave. I am in need of you. But you just close your eyes and walk away….."

Luna

I couldn't believe my eyes. Why was I walking outside into yet another insane situation, when I could be halfway to my bedroom and seconds away from sexual pleasure? I stood there silent in disbelief watching all of this unfold in slow motion, still half naked under my jacket. I was so ready to kill them both with my bare hands; but since I wasn't about prison life, I choose to kill them with my eyes instead. Dev walked slowly up the sidewalk towards my entrance, practically dragging my cousin, who could barely stand up straight in her stilettos'. Dev looked both embarrassed and ashamed, but not at all innocent. It was as if he was embarrassed to be dragging a drunk woman up a side walk, and ashamed that he was allowing her to ruin his outfit by getting all sorts of her random bodily fluids on him. I'm sure having a drunk girl he barely knew drool all over him was his idea of a living hell. The only thing to make things worse in his mind, would be if she threw up all the liquor she worked so hard to get down, all over him.

I could see him slowing shaking his head through the refrain of the streetlights, as he stopped only a few feet away from me. He held her with both arms trying to keep my cousin from falling flat onto her face. "I can't believe this shit!" I say to no one in particular. In my frustration and disbelief I throw my arms open wide, as if I was hoping to catch a bit of reality falling from the sky. All I really did was allow Dev to see what I was trying to keep hidden under my jacket. I scowled, gritted my teeth, as I began to whisper angrily at them both. "What the hell Dev? What the fuck is this? What are you doing at my house with my clearly drunk ass cousin this time of night? You should have taken her drunk ass back to her house. Why would you think this shit is okay?" Dev turned up the corner of his mouth as if he was ready to tell me where in the world I could go, and just how to get there. He looked me up and down quickly, raised his finger to my face, and began to burst out in pure rage. "BIH…" He stopped, put his hand up as if to calm himself down before he could finish the word, then continued. "Listen, I don't want to be here AT ALL. But I was at a club, I was chilling with my boys at the bar, and I saw your cousin getting pretty wild, AND getting pretty fucking wasted. I ignored her for a little while, cause her dumb shit ain't none of my business. Then I saw some dudes pushing up on her, reaching in her bag whenever her so called friends walked away. You know what, I could have let them run a train ran on her drunk ass, but I didn't. I was actually kinda worried when I saw that she decided to take her keys out, as if she would just drive home, clearly intoxicated, potentially killing herself or someone else. So being a nice guy, I drove her over here in her car, and my boy is waiting in the car for me to roll out. So goodnight Luna, best of luck with your drunk ass cousin!" He said in a dry monotone voice, dropping my cousin into my arms, then pushed past me to walk away. The anger boiled inside of me as I stood there just fuming. I wasn't going to let him go so easily. So I sat Apryl in a whicker chair I kept on my front porch, then rushed down the path after him. I caught up to him halfway down the sidewalk, then walked around to his face attempting to stop him in his tracks. Just as I was reaching out, he began putting up his hands, as if to keep me from touching his body. I started to getting angrier by the second. "No NO DEV. You need to take her with you. I have things to do tonight, and sobering her up is not my responsibility, nor was it in my plans. Yo this is serious. Take her home, or take her to one of her friends. I don't care where you take her, but you won't leave her here." The words tasted horrible falling off my lips as I said them, and I felt bad for not being willing to be a better cousin to Apryl. The truth still remained, that I was in no mood to be a savior tonight, especially when I knew this was her normal weekend behavior. She was young, and always ready to party. So drunk Apryl, is regular Apryl. Not to mention, Apryl never went out alone. She more than likely came to the club with a few friends; so his bullshit idea of bringing her over here, sounded more like a ploy to check up on me, and see if he could still get lucky one last time. Only problem was, he must have noticed by my attire, someone else was getting lucky with me tonight, just not him. Dev clearly was in the mood to continue any type of conversation with me, but I don't care, Apryl is his problem right now, not mine.

We were screaming at each other back and forth, and now the night air was getting cooler, but it still felt good enough for me to take the jacket off that was barely hanging on at this point. So much had transpired in such a short amount of time, that I'm sure my neighbors were getting concerned about my choice of friends and family. Dev tried to push me out of his way, so that he could head back towards the lot, when a deep voice came from behind him. "Woah, woah, woah there homie. Be careful how you handle the lady." Terri must have had come outside at some point to see what was going on, and helped my cousin into the house. I'm not sure how long he had been standing there, but he definitely didn't look happy to see Dev and I talking. It was at that moment that I realized just how different Dev and Terri really were. Not just as individuals, but in body type and demeanor. With Dev, I never felt secure, and protected when we went out. With Terri, I immediately felt that he was there to look out for me, and that he wouldn't let anyone hurt me. Now Terri was only a couple inches taller than Dev, but in confidence, strength, and swag, he seemed to tower over him. Dev stopped walking towards the parking lot when he heard Terri speaking to him, and had a look of intrigue on his face to see the man who was potentially his replacement. He stood there sizing Terri up, not sure where he remembered him from, but knew he looked familiar. Dev was probably hoping to find me home alone tonight, looking a mess, and possibly falling apart over our recent break up. Now seeing Terri, this strong handsome man walking towards us, as if he was staking claim to me, had to be an unexpected surprise for Dev. Terri barked out again. "I said be careful how you handle her my man." I started to walk to the other side of Dev, hoping to be in the middle of the two of them in case something more serious jumped off. Dev laughed a little, then looked at me pointing at Terri. "Haha, so this is number two huh? My replacement? Okay, Luna. Like I said, best of luck, and both of y'all can have a good night… Buh

BYE!" Dev waved us both off, as he turned once again and started to walk away. Terri reached around me and forcefully grabbed Dev's shoulder. "Yo first of all, like I said watch how you talk to her. Second you really ain't about to clown me as if I'm not standing here B. Not when I know yo punk ass tried to come over here under this false pretense of being a good guy. Clearly your plan failed, cause you were hoping to catch Luna here alone, and possibly see if you could get lucky. And your fucked up friend was probably hoping to maybe get lucky with her cousin. I bet that's why he so called followed you over in your car. I know how you roll. You're bitch made, and that's what boys like you do. Scheme on innocent women." Terri ranted, and I for one agreed. It did sound like something Dev and his idiot friends would have concocted, to prey on some other innocent girls. Terri continued. "So go ahead and take your sorry ass back to that 2000 piece of shit ride your friend followed you here in, and I'll take care of both of these ladies tonight." I stood back with a curious look on my face after hearing Terri's last comment. In my mind, I know he meant something totally different, it just came out as if he were planning to sleep with both my cousin and I tonight, so I frowned up my face. Dev quickly shot back, raising his hand and pointing all his fingers towards Terri's face. "Man FUCK YOU! You and Luna's crazy ass can have each other. I just told you I'm out. Conversation over bitch." But before I could stop him, Terri pulled back with his right arm, and threw a hard blow into Dev's, face knocking him to the ground. Within seconds, the two were rolling around between the sidewalk and foliage like two wild animals trying to kill each other with their bare hands. Terri was giving Dev a good old fashion ass whooping. Dev, grunting and growling, never fully able to gain his balance long enough to send any shots back, tried his best to land a solid punch. After about ten seconds or so, Wes, Dev's friend sitting in the car, ran over to pull Terri off. "Get off me bruh." Yelled Terri. I jumped in and pushed Terri back towards my house, and told Dev to hurry up and leave. Dev stood up after a few moments, and began to head towards the lot. Before he got in the car, Dev shouted out in our direction again. "Hope you enjoy that crazy ass bitch dog, and Luna remember that dude will never be me. I'll never be with your dumb ass again." I stood there puzzled as to why he thought that him not taking me back would concern me. So I shouted. "Please don't ever do me any favors by taking me back. What you can do, is take your wack ass home, and tomorrow you and your friend should hit the gym for practice. Would hate to see you get your ass whooped by a crazy bitch like me, right after you got your ass handed to you by my man." I smiled after I referred to Terri as my man. I never thought I would say Terri was my man, but it felt so natural coming out of my mouth, so I just rolled with it. Once we got back inside my house, Terri and I were reeling with excitement. My cousin had drifted off to sleep without missing a beat. Terri grabbed the small of my back, pulled me into his chest, and began passionately kissing me. A rush of heat covered over my skin. He picked me up, as I wrapped my legs around his waist, and he walked me upstairs to the bedroom. Must have been something about the adrenaline rush that had both of us steaming with passion and excitement. I'm not sure why, but the fight turned us both on; and that night we didn't make love, we made magnificent.

- Ohh how good it is, to feel loved in return. -

Chapter 5
Sometimes tomorrow isn't a brighter day

I'm so tired of waking up like this? In this body, with this mind full of distress. Unless I can find another way to be, I'm afraid this sorrow, will remain my reality. Tomorrow will be better, if I try.

Luna

It had been four days since the whole late night escapade with Dev, and Terri. Well, it was more like a melodramatic late night special on tv. While my cousin Apryl was passed out on the couch, Terri and I were knocking pictures off the wall in my bedroom. After our sweet sexual encounter, Terri and I decided we needed to determine what exactly we were doing in this relationship, or situationship we started to entertain. The morning after, Apryl must have woke up wondering where the hell she was, and how the hell she ended up at my place, versus that of some sexy bachelor who could've been her next meal ticket. It never ceased to amaze me that she was always able to find a man who was willing to be her Mr. Money Bags. Yet here I was still having my niave princess fairytale fantasy, of hoping to find my happily ever after with some sexy Prince Charming who had good credit, all his real teeth, and a Benz parked outside his mansion would be nice too. Nevertheless, finding this King Adonis, was apparently harder than finding a tooth in a mound of tic-tacs. Apryl left out the house before Terri and I came down for breakfast, so they were never really formally introduced. Probably for the best. She can be a bit much to deal with.

Days past, and now that I was back to my regular life, I was also back to my regular destructive thoughts. Tiana and I usually met for coffee or breakfast before my first meeting of the day, seeing how we worked in the same building. I slouched down in my chair and threw my head back, as if I were exhausted physically and mentally. "Guurrrllllll, why is this so hard? I mean, I like Terri and all, but sometimes he's too laid back for me to really read, ya know. I can never tell what he's thinking. He's all, yeah I'm cool with it, or nah it's not a big deal. I get the impression that he is just coasting along in our friendship doing the bear minimum, but hoping for maximum results. He says let's just take things easy, let things flow naturally. It's easy enough to just say we'll let things flow; but let's be real, I could be flowing right into the sewer." I finally exhale, sip on my mango berry smoothie, and wait for her response. "Stop playing around Lu. You know what he wants" Tiana smirks as she raises both eyebrows fast again and again. "That man wants some good head most days, and the other days, he wants to Netflix and chill with a bowl of vodka soaked fruit. HAHA!" She puts up her hand as if expecting a high five. I wasn't in support of her lame ass joke. So I give her the, bitch bye face, and shoot her the side eye so hard that my entire face became distorted. "T, stop it. No for real cut the jokes out. I'm Serious! What if this is about to be a huge waste of time just like the rest of them? What if all I'm getting out of this relationship is another broken heart, and worst credit?" I say jokingly, thinking back on the time when that asshole De'shawn stole my credit card, and raked up almost a thousand dollars in charges. That was a low point in my life for sure. She disregarded everything I'm rambling about, and responds calmly, knowing that I needed a soft gentle hand right now. "I think, that you THINK, too much. Let this situation evolve as it may. Over the course of time he will show you exactly who he is. He will let you know what kind of man he is, what he's willing to do, and what he's able to do for you. Point is, you have to give people the opportunity to fail, before you just completely write them off as failures." Tiana said in her Oprah, I know what I'm talking about cause I'm brilliant voice. As deep and philosophical as that shit was, I could only listen and agree. "You're right T, you are right. But you already know, I don't have time to waste. I'm getting older and my I can practically feel my eggs drying up inside of me." We both laugh heartily, then I immediately remembered that I had to get back to work, so I can't sit here forever. I quickly interrupt the laughter and ask "Ohhh snap, what time is it?" Searching for my phone to check the time, since I have a meeting at 9AM, and we came down to the juice bar at 8:30AM. I find my cell, and noticed that I had a text, and missed call.

Missed Call: Terri. SMS: Terri: *Did I say or do something wrong? I've been calling and texting u... Where u at?*

He usually doesn't have much to say, now all of a sudden he's calling and texting me all the time. I chalked it up to him being a man and wanting to keep his sex options open. Typically our conversations on the phone, or via text last just as long as they did the other night; a few quick minutes. Good thing our conversation was the only thing that lasted a few quick minutes. "Lu...Lu.... Luna! What time is it? You just stopped mid-sentence like you're a zombie or something. Do you need to go?" She said slowly as if I weren't capable of understanding her. "Yeah I do have to go, it's fifteen till. I stopped because I got a text. Terri, sent me a text is what I mean." I blow air out as if so unsure of what to do. "I'm just confused about everything, all of this feels like a mistake. I don't think this situation is going anywhere good. Please don't tell anyone I'm dating him." Rolling her eyes as if she did not want to be involved in any secrets I had. Then she said something that stopped me dead in my tracks. "You should stop thinking so much!"

If I'm being honest with myself; I can't stop thinking about the signs, the unsure feelings, just everything. It's because of not thinking, when I followed my heart, that I've gotten hurt the most.

Dev

I tapped my pen on my desk again and again, over and over as if I've developed some type of nervous tick. Without warning, I was snapped back into reality, when my coworker Chuck peered over the wall of my cubical and asked what I was doing for lunch. "Oh, hey Charlie. You know what man, I actually do have plans for lunch, but thanks for asking. I'll take you up on that lunch another day aight?" I tried to hurry him off, knowing I really didn't plans, but I also don't owe anyone an explanation about where I go, or what I do on my lunch break. I was planning to sneak out of the office to go home, hoping to avoid running into Luna's psychotic ass, since she worked across the street from my office building. In all five years that I have been working here, never have I been so introverted, and aloof. Bridgeton is by all accounts a small midwest town, and everyone knows someone who knows someone else who knows your ex. I want so desperately to put Luna, and that relationship as far behind me as I possibly can, so for now I gotta creep off every day to get some type of break. After waiting a few minutes for Charles to leave out, I lock my computer, check my phone for the time, and shuffle off to the parking garage. As I'm sneaking away, I feel my cellphone vibrating in my pocket, so I check to see who's messaging me during this time of day.

HOOK-UP: M-Sexy *"Hey you, how's your day going?"*

This sexy little thing I've been following on this dating app for the last three days, finally hit me up. Seeing how the other night at Luna's house went terribly wrong, I had to get back out there to see what easy piece of ass I could score, with the least amount of effort of course. So getting onto "Hook-Up", an app known for basically meeting strangers for sex, seemed like the most logical thing to do. I like to think I treat women right, but that was only if a woman is willing to fully submit herself to me. Women today don't seem to know their place; which is second to a man. All my friends agree with me. If you think of how the world was created, man first, then woman second. It only stands to reason that a real woman shouldn't have all that mouth that Luna has. She doesn't try to make more money than her man, nor does she go off and do things on her own without consulting her man first. Pretty much all of the things that Luna did, which got under my skin on a daily basis. "Ugghhh", I growled angrily thinking of Luna again, but then shook off all the annoying thoughts so that I could come up with something cleaver to say to Ms. M-Sexy. I looked back at my phone and sent a message hoping to keep here engaged in the general conversation.

"Oh it's just another day in the office with the same old same. What about you? What's going on Ms. sexy?"

As soon as I pressed send, almost instantly I got a response. "Damn, That was fast!" I think aloud. Her response was exactly what I was praying for.

HOOK-UP: M-Sexy: *"I'm trying to come hang out with you at your place tonight. If you can be free, I can head your way at 9:30."*

She cut straight to the chase, and I'm not sure if I like it, or if I love it? I grinned from ear to ear as I was getting into the car. We started going back and forth in playful sexual banter, wasting no time to respond about tonight. I tell her that I live in the new condos by the Palace Mall, and send her my cell phone number so that she can text me off of the app. Woohoohoo! I shrieked out loud like an excited school boy. What better way to get over an old girl, than by getting on top of a new one. Who said getting ass is hard. The internet has helped every man like myself get access to the easiest women on the planet, and right now after having things so hard with Luna for the last six months, all I need is something easy.

10:45PM

To: M-Sexy: *"Hey what time did you think you'll be coming by? I have to work tomorrow. I'm not gonna be able to stay up too late with you."*

With each passing minute I was becoming more annoyed by the fact that this girl was obviously playing games. Just as I started to think that she had stood me up, I hear a knock at the door. "Who is it?" I refuse to get up from the couch, until I know exactly who is at the door. "It's me! Marina." She said as I hear a sweet innocent voice from behind the large dark wooden condo door. My attitude immediately changed. Finally my dream of getting something new was almost a reality. Now all I have to do is let her inside the house, and convince her to take her clothes off. I jumped up and straightened myself out, then rush towards the door. Before I answer, I quickly set the mood with a few romantic lights, and yelling at my voice automated speaker system to play my night time playlist; which was really just more background noise encouraging getting her panties off. I stop by the fridge to grab a bottle of wine I had chilling since 7:30, Then I slowly stroll across the room to open the door. When Marina walked in, she took my breath away. She looked unbelievably amazing. On her picture she looked like she was one of those naturally beautiful people in the world. In person, my first impression is that she looks way too good to be true. Wearing a simple white top, blue pencil skirt, and white and blue sneakers to match. Her large perky breast, jiggled softly, as they peered out of her top, almost as if she was intentionally trying to draw me into them. Her legs were curvy, and fit. Her light brown skin complimented by her dark brown hair, which fell softly on her shoulders, in a long straight bob hairstyle. No doubt, she is amazingly beautiful, and I can't wait to see what kind of freak she was trying to be for me tonight.

The room was filled with smell of clean linen candles, as I welcomed her inside, and began showing her around my place. I handed her a glass and asked if she would like some white zinfandel, hoping to take the edge off for both of us. After the brief tour, we headed back into the living room to take a seat on the couch. The conversation was dry and forced at first. Stirring about general topics like television and music, nothing really serious, because we both know what she came for. I asked if she had been on the app long, and she shook her head no, then took a long sip from her glass. Next thing I know, like a wild animal she reached down to unzip my pants, and began kissing all over me. "Thank the lord!" I was overjoyed she took the situation into her own hands, because I was wondering how long I would have to stall with the conversation talking about shit I cared nothing about. Since Marina was taking the initiative, it gave me a clear sign that she was about the action that I was about too. She slid down to the floor on her knees, pushed her hair out of her face, and took all of me into her mouth as fast as she could. Again and again she until I was fully aroused and ready to lose myself completely. I had to slow her down, because I was about to let go, but she must've noticed that I was pretty excited, since she popped up and began to undress from head to toe. "Where did you come from?" I asked in a sexual trance. It really didn't matter where she came from, she was here now, and doing exactly what I wanted. We never made it to the bedroom; instead we rolled around on the couch and floor for another 30 minutes until I exploded with pleasure. Just like that, as soon as the evening had started, it had ended just as fast.

I rolled over on the floor to lie on my back, looking up towards the vaulted ceilings. "Phew.. ohh girl you're a wild one. Where did you learn that little twist thing you did?" We both laughed. "You know what, don't even answer that. I kinda want to know, but kinda don't want to know either." We both laughed as she reached over my torso, which startled me for a moment, since I thought she was trying to get me geared up for round two, and I wasn't quiet ready yet. Instead she grabbed her phone, since we heard it buzzing a few times in between our heaving and moaning. The room seemed a little darker now, which made the light from her phone seem much brighter than it really was. I wasn't really trying to look over her shoulder, but I caught a glimpse of what I was sure was Luna's new mans face on Marina's cellphone. Unable to hold back my disgust, I made a loud sucking noise with my teeth. "Wait a minute, wait a minute. What's that guy's name? And how do you know him?" She looked at me confused as to why I would be questioning her about who was on her phone, but she responded anyway. "Ohh this? That's my older brother Terri. He's just checking on me." She said praying that they didn't know each other. "Hold up... That guy is your older brother? HA! That dude tried to fight me last week over this chick, rather my ex, cause the bitch is crazy. Anyway, it doesn't matter, I just think he has the wrong idea about me, but I don't know the guy. So how much older is he?" I said hoping to change the subject, and hoping to avoid discussing the fight. Now Marina was more confused than ever. Terri never gets into fights, and how did they even meet, let alone date the same girl. Without hesitation she says that she's almost fifteen years younger than Terri, but catches herself and tries to act like she's joking about the age difference, only it was too late. I started processing what she said. "Oh ok cool, cool... but umm, hold up; that's a big age gap..... Wait, hold on, fifteen years right? And your bother is around my age like thirty, and if you're fifteen years young then the two of us, how old are you?" I was beginning to freak out, and my fear was quickly validated. Marina noticed the change in my tone, and the look of terror on my face, so she tries to calm me down as quickly as she can. "Don't get mad, and promise not to hold this against me, but I'm 16 and a half! But I'm really mature for my age. You saw that tonight! I won't tell anybody what we did I promise." I can't believe what I'm hearing. I jump up, fully naked, and start to experience my first ever panic attack. Reality was setting in, and I realized that if anyone finds out about tonight, my life will be all the way over. "OMG, you bitch.. You Stupid bitch... I'm so Fucked!"

-   Hello... Hello? We're sorry the person you're trying to reach is gone!-

Chapter 6

Decisions will be made

In the moonlight, I come alive. I breathe with a new set of lungs. I don't creep through the shadows, and I don't lurk in the corners, because in the dark a new life has begun. I don't look for the coverings, I don't find the cloaks to shield me. I stand bold and tall around thee, because I have nothing to fear! The darkness is so honest, so real, so free, so true. I will never go quietly into it, for in the darkness, my voice the world can finally hear!

Luna

"Do you think our breakup is my fault? I mean, what could I have done differently to have kept my relationship going?" I asked Alton as we ate sushi at our favorite restaurant. He stared at me annoyingly as if he didn't want to answer the question. One, he knew it was a ridiculous question, and two he had just shoved a large piece of sushi into his mouth. He held his finger up in the air as if to say one second. After he was able to chew, and eventually safely swallow his food, he slowly began to answer my question. "Well…. were you willing to be his personal slut at all times, deal with him only helping you when and how he wanted, or be willing to be ignored when he wanted to hang out with his boys? How about, were you willing to allow him to make all the decisions in your life, about how and when you did things? I mean as long as you're okay with that, I would suggest you go back now, and beg him for his forgiveness. Ohh, but please go back wearing nothing but some high heels and a smile; I'm sure he'll be willing to hear you out if you show up like that." He smirked then rolled his eyes, before laughing under his breath. I wasn't amused, and was really hoping for an answer I could use. "Come on, he wasn't all bad. Remember the time he bought me breakfast and flowers to work?" "Psht. But then later that day, didn't he come over to your house, saying that you should've be on all fours ready for him, because he was so nice to you that day? So maybe I have a point." I shrugged him off. "Bitch, of course I have a point! We don't see the ridiculousness of our relationships, or situations, when we are caught up in them. From the beginning of your relationship, anyone could see that he was more concerned with seeking approval from his friends, then making sure he was doing right by you. That doesn't mean that he was a bad guy, he just needs to grow up, OR, find someone who is willing to accept his shit the way he's willing to give it." Damnit, I thought. Alton, along with many of my other close friends were right. Dev was only a good boyfriend when he wanted to be, and most other times he was absent and doing what he wanted. He only celebrated my special events when HE wanted to, and never when it was important for me. Our relationship was mostly about conditions; on the condition that he was ready, and on the condition that if he did something for me, then I had to do exactly what he wanted to keep him "happy". If I really took a true inventory of our situation, things were getting bad fast. In the last few months we began to argue so frequently that we hated being around each other. There I was, trying to fight for equal footing, love, and value in our relationship the way I needed it, but that wasn't something he was ever going to give me.

We finished our sushi, and headed towards the parking lot, when my phone buzzed and I saw a text from Terri.

SMS: T: *I miss you beautiful. Can we get together soon? Let me know.*

I smiled unconsciously, and Alton quickly took notice. "Who got you grinning like a house cat?" Alton asked staring at me inquisitively. "Ohh, no. It's nobody. Somebody just sent a picture of some male model. You know people on social media, that's all." I definitely didn't want him to know I was seeing someone else so soon. Terri had to be my little secret until I was in a space to be willing to be vulnerable again. Dev had my nose so wide open for so long, that when he left me looking like a damn fool in the end, I promised myself to never go through that again. I'm going to make sure Dev regrets playing with a woman's heart, but in the interim, I want to enjoy getting some good love and attention from a new man.

Dev

"You gotta go… RIGHT NOW! RIGHT NOW!" I yelled at Marina, as I rushed about the room tossing any clothes I could find in her direction. I couldn't even see straight, mostly through terrified eyes as though someone was going to know that I had just slept with a minor. Also because I know if her brother finds out, I'm equally fucked, because Terri already hated me over another stupid bitch. Marina was moving in slow motion, swatting clothes out of her face as they were coming at her fast and furiously. "Why are you freaking out, my age doesn't change who I am as person." Marina was now beginning to sound stupid as fuck, as she was slowly get dressed. "I'll be 17 in 2 weeks, geez. I know I said 15 years but it's really only like 12. He has a different mom, and we don't even live together." I look at her like she was an idiot. I don't care if he lived in another galaxy, she was a minor, and he would kill me, along with the police if they find out. "Besides my brother, we both had fun tonight, didn't we?" She said in a skirt and bra as she started to seductively walk over towards me. I hope she doesn't think her sex appeal would distract me from this clearly intense situation. "I don't care if your birthday is tomorrow, you are still a child, and I will go to jail for this shit. Bitch I have a life, and you could literally ruin it. Do you get that?" I was still freaking out, screaming so loud and not paying attention that my roommate Sherrod was coming into the house through our back door. As we continued to get dressed, I finally heard Sherrod walking towards us in the other room. "YoYoYo Dev? You in there bro?" I froze, reached my arm across her chest as if to tell her to be still, then gestured to Marina to not say a word. "Yeah bro, I'm in here but I got company, give us one second, cause…" I paused before continuing because I couldn't figure out what to say next, then I quickly thought of a way to redirect him from coming in and seeing my "minor" problem. "Matter of fact. uhh just stop by your room while I let her out, then I'll come holla at you." Sherrod replied cool, then hurried up the stairs towards his room with what sounded like tons of bags. I took Marina to the door grabbing anything that remotely looked like it belonged to her. I didn't care if she took the television remote, as long as she was gone and never came back. Before I could close the door in her face, she reached out to me for a hug, but I backed away as if she was the bubonic plague. "Woah, girl are you crazy? I'm never touching you again. What happened here was a

37

mistake, and now that I know, it's never gonna happen again. Don't call me or message me ever again." I whispered, knowing my words were harsh, but that was the only way I knew how to directly tell her that we aren't going to be a thing, and that this was NEVER going to be repeated. "I liked you D, this really hurts. But if you change your mind, call me." She turned to walk away and I quickly closed the door on her, and hopefully to the horrific mistake that I made.

As I was about to call out to Sherrod, when I noticed that he was standing closer than I would've liked to our front door. I tried to plaster a fake smile of enjoyment on my face, to keep him from knowing that I was a potential sexual predator. "Hey Sherrod, what's good B?" I asked as I walked to the kitchen and opened the fridge to look for something strong to drink. "Man, I'm good, but you the one out here winning! I saw that ass walk outta here. That's what I'm talking about!" He said has he walked over to give me a pound on my fist in agreement with how amazingly sexy Marina was. I couldn't deny that she was a beautiful young lady. It was the fact that she was a YOUNG lady that concerned me the most. Despite her age, the sex was amazing, the body was right, but I am not one of those dudes who says age ain't nothing but a number. I know those guys, they're the pervs in my old neighborhood, or my uncle Bunky. Nonetheless, I ain't never been one of them, and I'm not gonna start now. Sherrod continued to talk about her for another minute or two, before I changed the subject to ask who was his most recent freak. "Awe man, you know I had to expand my scope, because I've basically run through most of the hoes around here. I changed my profile to say I lived two hours north. I found a few chicks who look promising. So I went to the mall to get some new swag so I can meet up with a few prospects tomorrow and the next day." I nod my head in agreement, secretly wishing I could be more like him. He never had to take women out, he never let them stay the night, he didn't even have to really speak to them. All he had to do was wear his clothes, talk a good game, and next thing you know, they were smashing, and not long after that, he was dashing. Sherrod was the man all men secretly envied. I guess a part of me treated most of these hoes too well. But after tonight, all that shit's about to change.

Luna

Terri and I decided to get dinner, so that we could discuss what we were feeling for one another. I'm not really convinced that men have feelings, and right now my feelings are rather diluted. Hurt is a real disorder, and I was suffering. I sat in the middle of my bedroom floor meditating and repeating my personal mantra. "I am beautiful, stronger than I was before, more powerful than anything that comes up against me. I am the greatest of all time." I repeat it again and again trying to convince my subconscious mind that I am all these wonderful things. I hear my phone vibrate, and snap out of my wonder woman trance, because I don't want to be late for my first official public date with Terri. Not public like around where we live. Of course not. I'm not ready for the world to see me with a man I like. He planned to pick me up from my house so that we can go forty five minutes south of Bridgeton, where people don't know me, and I can relax and let me hair down.

Spivey is the fanciest seafood restaurant practically in the state. I was rather impressed that he decided to bring me here for our first official date. We ordered wine, and appetizers, and began talking like we never have before. I guess all this time of him being my friend, had me talking to him like a brother, and less like a lover.

"Can you name one thing that you love to do, and would do every day if money was of no concern?" Terri asked me as I started to take another bite of my Cajun shrimp pasta. I choke a little, because his question was coming out of nowhere, and I wasn't in the mood for corny date questions. I sip my wine then speak. "Well I love working with families, and inner city kids, so I guess I would to start a non-profit program to provide resources and educational programs for them." He smiled genuinely, and started to ask more questions about my dreams and ambitions. We were really on a full fledge date. We flirted back and forth, cracked silly jokes, and talked about what we wanted for the future throughout the night. We were having such a wonderful time, and everything was so natural. We finished our dinner, then decided to share a desert before heading home. "Luna, why have we waited so long to do this?

We been friends, we know a lot about one another, so what was the problem? Oh yeah that's right, you have a fascination with fuck boys." I laughed sarcastically, then I used my fork to accidently push some chocolate cake onto his cheek. "hahahaha, now the jokes on you." I reached for my napkin to help clean off his face, but he reached for my hand for what I thought was his chance to assist me in the cleaning effort, instead he pulled the back of my hand towards his mouth and kissed it passionately. For a moment I started to melt inside, but something strange stopped me. I thought to myself that this was all just a game, and maybe he was trying to pull another Dev, which meant setting myself up for failure all over again. I let him finish kissing my hand, I blushed and looked down as if I were embarrassed. "Terri, I'm having such a great time with you, and I truly love whatever this is we're doing here." I said circling my hands in the air as if to say we were in some type of weird bubble. "Buuutttt what? I know there's a but coming Lu, you may as well spit it out. And for some odd reason I feel like I'm gonna be put in the same bucket as some piece of shit we both don't like." Terri said with a serious undertone. I laughed quickly then went on. "It's not that, I just don't know if I'm ready for a relationship." He stopped me. "Luna. We can go as fast, or as slow as you want. I just want to be with you. I want to see you in the morning, and I want to hold you at night. I want to kiss your tears when you cry. I want to be there for the good times, and the bad. I'm your friend first, and everything else second. Okay?" Terri's response was so genuine, something I hadn't heard from anyone in a long time, and it brought peace to my heart. "Terri.. Dammit, I Freaking heart you man…." I said making a heart gesture using both of my hands. We both laughed as he paid the check, and we headed towards the door. Once we got back to my house, he gently kissed me goodnight, and he told me that he'd call me as soon as he could tomorrow, because he was going out of town for work. I didn't know what was happening with Terri and I; but I was beginning to like it, and that's all that matters right now.

Dev

Friday

I decided that because of everything that happened last night, I just couldn't bring myself to go into the office, so I called my supervisor and told her that I needed to take a personal day. I just had to clear my head, and get over what all went down. Buzz, buzz, buzz.

Marina had continued to text me a few times since last night. Both apologizing for misleading me, and saying that it was a mistake to not tell me her age in the beginning. She calls it misleading, but it wasn't just being mislead, this bitch flat out lied. I continued to ignore her messages, I scrolled through her page on the dating app again. How could I have missed it, I thought? I mean the convo was pretty dry, and yeah I wasn't really asking a lot of deep questions, so is this on me? No, it's on her. I tried to convince myself that I was the victim, and there should be some type of "victims of misleading bitches" recovery group I could attend somewhere. She texted again a simple *"Can we talk please?"* Man this bitch is crazy if she thinks we're going to talk. I'm not gonna waste my time, and risk potentially getting caught up. I said out loud. The conclusion is this; Marina was a terrible accident that I can never deal with again. Before I knew anything about her age, the sex was amazing. I mean I have never felt so good before. "What if we just… No no I can't, not only is it morally wrong, it's fucking illegal." I'm talking to myself as if I needed to consider things on both sides. I have to stop thinking about the curve of her hips, or about how she let me do whatever I wanted without complaint. Buzz, buzz, buzz. My cell starts going off I look down to see a naked picture of Marina from the neck down. Smart, and sexy I thought. No, I need to stop her. I can never do this again. Sherrod walks in the room as I try to put down my phone from the explicit picture of what I know is considered child porn on my phone. "Naw, dude, don't try to hide that. Shorty is sexy as hell, I seen that picture. So you think you gonna break that off again?" Sherrod asked as he came into the room, and sat on the other end of the sofa. He picked up the remote before asking if he could change the channel on the television, that was apparently watching me. He didn't know anything about her age, all he saw was a big butt and a smile. If I could keep all of this a secret, what's the problem with just getting some ass from time to

41

time. I hesitated to answer, but finally came to a conclusion. "You know what bro…. I have too. That ass was just too good."

- A man who lacks morality, lacks a soul…-

Chapter 7

Considering Options

If you saw a rainbow today, you saw my smile. If you heard a bird sing in the morning; you've heard my voice, even just for a little while. If you felt the coolness of the evening breeze, I was breathing in your direction. But if you ignored all these things I have given to you; then you have never felt my true love and affection.

Luna

"Terri you are so silly, stop it. I miss you so much babe, when are you coming back to see me?" She giggled on the other end of the phone as he continued to laugh and crack jokes. Terri couldn't believe it, he was really in love with this woman. Although things may have been moving quickly, he wanted to make sure he let her know just how he felt. He told himself that this situation was just too perfect to mess up. He let out a loud whoohoohoo, deep down laughing sound, as if he was trying to calm down enough in order to speak. "You know, I'm so glad that you're in my life right now. And I know it hasn't been very long that we've started this thing that we're doing, but it just feels right. Don't judge me, but I think… I think I love you." She paused for a second, unsure if she was rushing by responding to his statement in agreement. Then he breaks the silence to make sure she was still on the line. "Hello, baby? Baby are you still there?" "Yeah, babe sorry, I'm here. I love you too T. I mean it. You make me so happy, and I was just surprised to hear that you feel that way about me already." He smiled in the phone before responding with a fake sigh of relief. "Phew. Girl. You had me worried for a second there. Thought I was gonna have to make a special trip over there to hold you down and cover you with kisses till you saw things my way." The left side of her mouth curved up into a seductive smirk. "I mean you can do whatever you feel is best. I'm not going to stop you from doing what you gotta do." He loved it when she started talking to him in her flirty girl voice.

Just as he was about to join in on the sexy foreplay, he saw a shadow walking towards his car, so he rushed her off the phone. "Hey babe, listen I'll call you later when I'm free, I'm actually about to go out with my friends, and they bugging me to get off the phone. But I love you." He waited to hear her say she loved him back before he hung up, then jumped out of the car to greet his date. "Luna, baby. WOW! You look amazing."

Terri was dressed in a navy blue button down shirt, covered by a dark grey cotton jacket, straight leg dark wash denim jeans, and a dark plaid fedora he had slightly tipped forward on his head. I looked him up and down thinking "DAMN he is so fine." Terri couldn't take his eyes off me as I slowly, and in a jokingly seductive way, walked towards him as he got out of the car. I decided that I didn't want to look too eager to see him tonight, so I wore a simple green halter dress, that just happened to hug all my curves in all the right places, you know that slutty good girl attire. But like I said, I'm don't want to come off too eager or thirsty, so I covered up with a sheer gold shawl, that I gracefully tied so that it draped down my shoulders and in the front of my chest. He struggled to speak again as he stood there with his mouth gapped open. "Girl… I'm uhhh. I mean, like… Well, I, don't know what else to say, you just look amazing!" I could tell Terri meant it, and it felt good to get that reaction from him. He stopped staring at me for a second, and looked as if he remembered something, and turned around to reach into his car. He rustled about for a second, then he handed me a huge bouquet of multicolored roses. "Oh my goodness Terri, they're beautiful! You're so sweet. Thank you babe." I leaned in to hug him around his neck before taking the flowers from his hands. I was taken aback by his kind gesture. Here I was just a week ago crying over a man who wouldn't love me like I wanted or needed. Now, here I am, standing outside of my house dressed in a sexy outfit, going out with an amazing guy who was right under my nose the whole time. "You know what? How lucky are you to have finally made it into my life? I mean after all these years of just being the best of friends, and now I may even let you be my main man." We both laughed at my fake English accent. Terri was nothing like Dev, and that's exactly what I wanted.

Dev

Sherrod leaned in to slap my hand excited at the notion of me sleeping with sexy ass Marina again. I couldn't bring myself to tell him the truth about her age, I doubt he would be so happy then. All I had to do was keep things casual with him, never letting on that I know much about her other than the fact that she has a fat ass, big titties, and is a freak. As a man, we never need to know details about hoes. It's the bitches we claim to fall for that we need to know details about. The bigger problem in this situation, was going to be making sure Marina was going to be able to keep her mouth shut, never telling anyone about what we're doing, especially her older brother. I figured I could finesse her over a romantic dinner at my place; bitches always loved that corny shit. So I asked Sherrod if he was going to be home at any point this weekend, so I could potentially see if I could invite Marina over without him possibly running into her again. I had to be very strategic about how I moved her in and out of the house. This situation was really going to test my maneuverability skills. "Yo Rod, what you got up this weekend? You bringing anything through?" I asked nonchalantly. "Actually I'm gonna head up north, this chick trying to impress ya boy by renting a cabin and buying dinners and shit. You think I'm gonna pass that up? NO! Problem is I don't know what to talk to her about for two days, so I'm gonna head up there late on Saturday, and make up something so I can come back before the game on Sunday. You know I'm not about the conversing shit wit hoes… feel me?" I shook my head in agreement. I hated talking, that's why whenever Luna tried to start one of her impossible deep ass conversations, I had to muster up an erection just so that I could try to convince her to put something in her mouth to shut the hell up. I responded to Sherrod making sure to stay involved in his weekend plans, not letting him know much about mine. "Yeah man, I feel you. But you have fun though, go handle your business." I said as I raised my eyebrows, suggesting business was more like smashing his latest conquest. "I'm supposed to be meeting some new little thing, so I may bring her back here and convince her to cook for me, so that I can keep my bread in my pocket. It's good you're going to be out, this way in case things get serious, I don't have to worry about interfering with your company too." He shook his head in agreement. Sherrod wasn't a man of many words, and I liked that about him. Nothing was ever too serious for him, he just went to work, came home, smashed a bunch of hoes, and was happy. That's why he's one of my best friends. We were handling our business as successful grown men, and had I not gotten sidetracked with that crazy bitch Luna, I probably wouldn't have wasted almost an entire year of my life with some chick who was all about saving the world, and not sucking my dick.

Later that day as I was laying in my bed staring up at the ceiling, I thought about what I was going to say to Marina. I got up to head to my bathroom, and began looking at the my reflection in the mirror. I wasn't sure if the man I wanted to be in the future, was really going to be okay with what I was about to get involved in now in my present life. I turned on the faucet and splashed cold water onto my face, then proceeded to go back to my bed and search for my phone. I didn't want to get Marina's hopes up, as if I liked her the way she claimed to like me. Instead I needed to convince her that I'm only trying to get some ass without commitment. Deep down on the inside, I felt dirty about asking a minor to sneak out of the house; but then I remembered how good I felt inside of her, how my body shook with each stroke, and with those thoughts alone, my little head won that fight. I started typing a text letting the words flow as if I were Sherrod trying to seduce some random chick.

SMS: *"Hey Marina, it's me Dev. Look we need to talk in person. How about we have dinner at my place Saturday night about nine-ish?"*

I waited a few minutes before considering telling her never mind, that I changed my mind, but she responded with.

SMS: DoNotAnswer: *"I can be there at 9:45. I have plans with some friends, and I can't sneak away until 9:15. I'm glad you came around though. Thanks for giving me a chance to explain."*

Please, PLEASE, don't send me any incriminating shit, like you're a child and I'm a creep for continuing to sleep with you. I was happy she didn't say anymore, so I sent a simple, aight, see you tomorrow. Going forward with her, everything had to be strategically mapped out. Maybe I can tell her I'm not looking for a serious relationship, or that I just got out of a situation that was stressful, or better yet, that by messing with her we can't be public, so why even make a commitment. Whatever I told her, had to sound convincing enough to make sure she kept her mouth shut, but also kept her legs open only for me. This was about to be a true test of my skills and abilities.

Luna

"So now that you know how I feel about you, and I know how you feel about me, why are we wasting our time with these games?" Terri asked me directly as the server brought him the check. We had already finished dinner, and were just hanging out talking over coffee. Terri was holding my hand on top of the table, as we were staring into each other's eyes. His question wasn't as easy to answer as I would have liked. So I pursed my lips up as if I was unsure how to answer. Finally I blurted out. "Fine Terri, what is it that you want for us? Didn't you previously say we could just continue to take our time as we discover more about one another, then we'll determine if we actually want more than friendship." I couldn't bring myself to admit that I wasn't ready for anything serious with anyone. All I wanted were kind words, and a warm body to lay next to me a few nights a week. Terri rolled his eyes before he began to speak. "Luna are you serious? Learn more about each other? We've been friends for years. Are you sure you aren't still caught up with Dev?" I quickly interrupted. "HELL NAW! I'm not worried about that asshole anymore." I had to close my eyes tightly and take a deep breath before going on. "I just don't want to jump into anything heavy right now. Plus I want to know that you are serious about what you and I are doing." He flared his nostrils, turned his eyes towards ceiling before gesturing with his hand as if to ask me, was it okay for him to speak yet. "Lu, I get that you're scared. I understand that he hurt you; but I care about you. To be honest, I don't think that I can really see my life without you in it. You're my friend, and now you're so much more than that. I just want you to really give this a chance." He leaned in and gently caressed my face and lifted my chin so that our eyes locked for a moment as he continued. "Listen, this is as much about me wanting to develop something real with you, as it is that I don't want to be used. So many women in the past have come into my life post a breakup, and I become this rebound guy that gets temporarily taken for a ride. And although so many men say they don't care about being used just for sex. It gets pretty shitty when you start to care about some of the women you're sleeping with. So, just as much as I promise to be careful with your heart; I also need you to consider that I'm invested in this relationship too, so be careful with mine." A relationship? So soon, with someone I've only ever known as a good friend. "Just give me a little more time Terri. Just a little bit more. Please?"

As we walked out of the restaurant hand in hand, I could tell that he really cared about me, and I couldn't deny that he's always been in my corner. He handed the valet his ticket, then turned to look me in the eyes, so I leaned in and passionately kissed him on the lips. As I backed away, just far enough so that he could hear me speak, I said, "I promise not to hurt you, but again; I need a little more time. For now, let's just say I'm 100% your girl without the title." He smiled then gave me a gentle peck in agreement. As we drove home, I noticed his phone illuminated a few times as he was getting text messages. One had the name mommy with a heart emoji as the picture. I smiled at the thought that he still calls his mother, mommy. I asked if he needed to call anyone back, if so it was okay while I was in the car, I would be quiet. He replied, "Naw, my mom is sick and I told her I would come by this weekend, I guess she can't wait till tomorrow to see me. You don't mind that I don't stay the night do you?" I waved him off, "Mind? That's your mom dude, what kind of woman do you think I am? Who gets mad at someone for going to help their mom? You can drop me off, and I'll catch up with you later when you're free." "Well you know I'm gonna take care of my "girl" first. I'm not leaving without showing you just how much I appreciate you stepping out with me looking so damn sexy tonight." He slide his hand up my thigh as he continued to steer the car with the other hand.

Once at my house, he closed and locked the door behind him, pulled me in close, kissed my lips as he was rubbing his strong hands all over my body. He continued to caress me passionately, then lifted my dress up, as he slowly lowered himself to the floor. I gasped aloud as he ripped off my thong and began tasting my precious jewel. "Thank you, thank you, thank you, thank you, thank you…." I repeated over and over again as if it were a chant. "You okay up there?" He said as he raised his eyes but never moving away from my waist. "Yeah, just really happy, don't stop, we're good." I said panting as if I had just finished a long run. Terri ravaged me for what seemed like ages, until my legs began to give way, and I felt like I was going to crumble to the floor. At that exact moment he lifted me up and continued to have his way with me. He knew just what to do, and my body had never felt so alive with anyone else. The chemistry we shared was unbelievable, and we both knew it. He could very well be the ONE. Who knows, Terri could be the last man I ever make love to. After we finished, he used the restroom, put his clothes back on kissed me as I was falling asleep. "See you later this weekend Lu." I thought I said goodbye to Terri, but who honestly knows, he put me out like a light with what we did. I rolled over and drifted off to a peaceful night's sleep.

SMS: Mommy: *"Hey babe, I'm on my way home. I hope you're keeping it ready for me. Love T"*

Dev

"Alright D, I'm heading out. Promise to do something I would do this weekend, like smash some hoes." Sherrod slaps my back playfully as he heads out the door for his weekend of being treated like a king by one of his many ladies. I knew I had a good chance of getting lucky tonight, but he would never know who my new reliable piece of ass is going to be. Again the less he knows about Marina, the better it is for all parties involved.

Soft love songs played in the background. I lit vanilla scented candles, and opened a few windows hoping to get a nice breeze flowing, since cooking warmed the house up more than I would have liked. I made the one recipe that I knew I couldn't mess up, Chicken Alfredo. I added some broccoli, garlic bread on the side, and had some soda chilling in the fridge; since I was already breaking one law, no need to break all others by giving alcohol to a minor. Plus, now that I know the truth, if she wanted to drink, she was going to have to supply her own liquor. Tonight was about setting the ground rules for what this situation was going to be. Today I was ready for her, and nothing was going to surprise me or catch me off guard again.

I heard a door close outside, and looked out the window to see her walking up towards my place. Before she could even knock on the door, I answered. As I expected, at first glance she took my breath away. Tonight she wore a knee-length skin-tight black dress, with some gold pumps that strapped around her ankles. "Where did you go with friends in that?" I asked confused, but pleased at how great she looked. She looked herself up and down and said "Ohh, this? I went to a party for my friend's birthday at this lounge on the east side of town. I always get in cause I know the bouncer. They stayed to party." She walked in and took a deep breath in. "Wow, you did say we were going to have dinner. I guess I didn't expect you to be so serious about it." She looked around as if hoping to see food sitting out already prepared. "Yeah I got you on dinner. Just go have a seat at the table, I'll bring out the food in a second. I only have soda tonight, is that cool?" Knowing we always have a stash of liquor, but she wasn't going to know that. "Yeah as long as it's dark cola, I have some rum I'll add to mine. You can have some of my liquor if you want to." She said so confidently as if it were no big deal for her to have a bottle of rum. Damn, this girl is really too much, I thought. "Uhh sure that's fine." I handed her a couple of glasses filled with a few cubes of ice, then I went back to making the dinner plates. Once I was done, I set the table and we began to eat.

I wasn't very hungry, since my stomach was flipping around, trying to figure out how to get this girl to commit to being a secret piece of ass for me. I started the conversation with something I really wanted to know about. "How was it that you are able to freely move about as if you're grown, but you're a teenager. I mean, if you don't mind me asking, where are your parents at?" She swallowed her bite, and began to speak. "Well, I basically just live with my dad. My mom has been very sick most of my life, and she goes in and out the hospital throughout the year. On top of my mom being sick, my dad works two jobs, so I hardly ever see him. Plus I'm the baby, so everybody lets me get away with practically anything. I have a car, and my older siblings always give me money, so I'm taken care of." Her story was sad, but perfect for our situation. She could do what she wanted without having to check in with anyone, and I could potentially keep getting what I wanted without ever having to commit. "Damn sorry to hear about your mom. Sounds like you just take care of yourself, but you're good though. I can tell you're really smart and mature." We both smiled at each other, as we kept eating. The food was good in my opinion. I can at least follow a recipe if nothing else. I took a swig of my rum and soda and finished my thought. "Well I won't continue to get into your personal life, I was just asking. Anyway, I wanted to invite you over tonight to apologize for how I acted the other day. You know I freaked out because of the age thing, but also cause I'm just getting out of a really bad relationship, and I'm kinda uneasy. Which is why I wanted to talk to you. Marina I'm not looking for another relationship. I joined the hook-up app, just to hook up. We can kick it and be cool, even hang out occasionally, but I can't give you anything, like ANYTHING other than that." I paused for a moment to let her speak. "D, I'm not trying to be your girl. Yeah I want friendship, and I like you. We both know I'm too young right now for anything serious. I'm only trying to feel good and escape my reality at home." I felt such a sense of relief to hear that she wasn't looking for love. So I took another risk, and asked her a very direct question. "So just to be clear, you still down with taking care of me though right?" As I pointed towards my crotch. "Yeah I'm definitely going to handle that." She said with a smile. Damn, who would've thought it was all going to be this simple.

- I am what I say I am. For the desires of my heart, will seep from my mouth.-

Chapter 8

Secrets from our past....

Tempered. Trained. Repetition.

Lies. Persuasion. Contradictions.

Instant. Patience. Wavered.

I am so much more than my description.

The history of Dev

1999....

"Happy Birthday my Lil Man! You're 10 Years old today." My mom said as she came crashing into my bedroom just as my alarm started to go off. I tried to roll over into the blanket not wanting her to see the huge grin on my face. "Mom, get out of here. You promised to let me sleep in for 10 more minutes today, cause it's my birthday." I groaned, but was glad she woke me up, I was excited to see what gifts she got for me since she had been working all those extra hours at the factory these last couple weeks. I just knew she was going to make sure this birthday was extra special. She laughed, leaned in to pull the blankets away, then began to smoother me with kisses, before pulling away and beginning to talk to me in a her baby voice. "Well I couldn't help myself, you're my first born baby, my only son, and I love you so much." We both laughed together, as she pulled the entire blanket off of the bed, jumped in, and began to tickle me furiously.

We stopped laughing as we felt a dark shadow, and a cold presence enter the room. "Donna? DONNA? What are you doing in here playing around, when you should be downstairs making breakfast? Leave him alone, and do what you're supposed to be doing. And DJ, while you're laughing, you need to get cha ass up and get dressed for school. I'm tired of seeing your face boy." My dad said sternly. We were used to him being so cold, since that was the only tone he used us most days. We paused for a second hoping he'd turn and walk away, but he didn't, instead he immediately barked back at us. "WHY ARE YOU STILL LOOKING AT ME? MOVE!" As loud as he yelled, it scared us so much that we jumped, and instantly went into action. Dad knew I hated being called DJ, especially since I wasn't his junior, but he did it because he said a man's son is always his junior, no matter if the names are the same or not. My dad didn't stay with us often, rumor had it that he had a couple other families in the town where we lived, and he frequently just hopped from house to house visiting all of his children and their mothers. I don't know if that's true, but I do know I have two other older siblings that my dad treats way better than me, and he's always treated my baby sister from my mom like a princess. I just don't think my dad likes me very much.

I rushed to get dressed, then met my mom downstairs in the kitchen. "So baby, what kind of cake do you want today?" My mom asked with her back to me, never looking up from the stove. She was intently focused on finishing breakfast, while my father showered and got ready for work. Most days when he was actually staying at our house, were filled with him screaming directives, taking mom's money, and always locking mom in the room to do whatever they did, while I had to watch over Ariyana my baby sister. Even though Ariyana is six, she's still a baby to me, but she was treated way better by daddy than I ever was. Today being my birthday, I hoped he remembered, and was nicer to me, because I'm always doing what he says without question or hesitation. I'm ten now, and I'm growing up, so he can't talk to me like a little boy anymore, I'm a pre-teen! "Hello, Earth to D, Earth to Dev. Boy you just went into a trance over there, could you even hear me?" Mom was smiling and holding a plate of fresh hot pancakes and sausage in front of my face. I reached out to grab it, and immediately covered everything with warm maple syrup. Shoving forkful after forkful into my mouth, I heard my dad coming down the stairs followed by my little sister, and both were laughing and giggling as though they had no cares in the world. As they walked into the kitchen, his smile soon faded as he seen me eating before him. "What the hell is this? Where's my plate? And the food better be hot." My mother quickly sat a large plate of hot breakfast in front of dad, as he sat across from me and began to eat. This was a regular weekday in my house, whenever dad was here.

Mom sat down after getting Ariyana some food, and began to drink some coffee. She cleared her throat trying to get dad's attention. He barely raised his head, just glanced at her through the corner of his eyes. She looked in my direction, then nodded towards the hall closet near the kitchen door. My dad began to speak without even looking up from his plate. "You can go in there if you want, but ain't shit in there but one thing." My mom's smile quickly faded and she became angry. "What do you mean ain't shit in there but ONE thing? It was filled with things just yesterday? Where did all the things go Arthur?" She jumped up and ran over to the closet only to find one box wrapped in happy birthday wrapping paper. I could hear her sigh a deep long sigh like she was disappointed. Only she turned around, walked towards my side of the table and handed the large box to me and calmly said "happy birthday baby." She kissed my head then whispered, "can you take your sister to your room for a few minutes, then I'll come get you guys for school, okay?" I replied "yes ma'am" got up, then we both walked towards the living room to head up the stairs towards my room. Before we were even mere steps out of the room, the screaming match began.

"This is some low shit, even for you Arthur. You took all his stuff for what? FOR WHAT? That was three weeks of overtime for me! The shoes, clothes, toys, what did you do with it? Ariyana's stuff is still here, only Dev's things are gone. Why? WHY? Why would you do this to your own child?" My mom was screaming through her tears. "Bitch I don't owe you no explanations. You spent too much money on him anyway, so I took some shit back. I needed two new tires for my truck." My dad screamed so loud that I'm sure the neighbors could hear. "TIRES, for your truck? You took our sons gifts to buy tires, for your truck? Are you fucking serious? You know what? JUST GET OUT!! I don't want to see you anymore." I heard what sounded like my dad kicking a chair from under the table, my mom gasped, then got quiet. "Bitch, I'll leave, when I'm ready to leave. I'm always gonna be the man of this house. Remember that." It remained oddly quiet downstairs for a few minutes, then I heard dad open the closet door again, and then walked across the living room to open the front door to leave for work. Before he walked out, he yelled to my mom, "Donna, I want steak for dinner." After that, dad yelled up the stairs "I love you Ariyana, and bye DJ." He closed the door, and I heard my mom throw dishes in the sink. I couldn't wait for him to leave again, just disappear and leave us alone. My mom was so weak whenever he was around, always doing whatever he said, acting like she was really scared of him; but she could be the toughest strongest person I knew whenever he was gone. I hated my dad, but also I love him so much. I only wish I knew what I could do to make him like me more.

2002....

It had been hours since I was able to either see, or speak to my mom. Earlier that morning, I was called to the principals office at school, then Ariyana and I were both taken to the downtown police station in the middle of the day. Our mom met us there, and hugged us tight before they told her that she needed to go with a thin Asian woman who introduced herself as a doctor, and that Ariyana was going to be taken with someone else for an exam. Everything was happening so fast, that I had no idea what happened, only that Ariyana was the focus, and that strange people claiming to be doctors and police were asking me about how my dad treated us at home.

After my mom and sister left, I was escorted into a small empty room with only a table and three chairs. It had no tv, was colder than I would have liked, and I could hear all the noise from the outside offices. After what felt like hours, a tall skinny White man, and heavyset messy looking White woman came into the room where I had been sitting. They brought me a soda and bag of chips. I looked up, felt a little off balance I guess because I was tired and hungry, so I was grateful for the snack. "Thanks. Can you tell me how long I have to be here please? I haven't talked to my mom in a long time, and I'm getting pretty tired." I said exhausted from all the excitement today. The woman pulls up a chair in front of me and sits down before looking at the man for confirmation to speak. "Well Dev.. It is Dev right? Your mom is waiting for you just up the hall, but before you go, we had just a couple more questions. I'm detective Pearson, and I specialize in child abuse cases. Do you know what child abuse means?" She asked like I was dumb. "Yeah, like when your parents beat you and stuff. My mom doesn't beat us, my dad don't either. He's just a jerk to me sometimes. But they don't hurt us at home, I promise. Can I go now?" She nodded her head softly before continuing.

55

"Well, there are other forms of abuse, like mental, and sexual. Have you experienced anything like that?" I shake my head fast, cause my dad don't touch me. "Has your sister ever said anything about your dad touching her in a bad way?" I was so confused, I felt like my head was starting to spin. "No… No, he wouldn't do that. My dad has grown up women to touch, he wouldn't…. He wouldn't." She started to say that Ariyana said that daddy touched her in her private parts. "What? He did what?" The man interjected and says how my dad has been accused of touching Ariyana and another little girl, and they wondered if he touched me the same way. "No, I said NO!" I began to cry, because when I thought about it, things had been strange with him and her for the last year or so. I told them how my dad would come around our house sometimes when we first came home from school. He would tell me to go to the store and get him some beer, and gave me enough money to get myself something too. He told me to take my time, and that he'd stay with Ariyana at home so that I didn't have to watch her at the store. But when I'd get back, he'd snatch his things, and hurry up and leave. She would just stay in her room, and sometimes I heard her crying, but she never said anything to me. I just didn't know. They finished taking notes, told me they'd be right back, and next the thing I know my mom had walked into the room. She looked like she had been crying for hours, makeup smeared all over her beautiful medium brown face. She leaned in to hug me, and held me so tight, and whispered "I am so sorry." When she pulled away I didn't look at her the same. I saw weakness, and desperation. She was everything I never wanted to be. She didn't protect us, she didn't stand up to him. She just let him hurt all of us, over and over. I hated her for that. As we left the station, I saw my dad being shoved in handcuffs in the opposite direction of where we were heading to go home. "I knew you wouldn't press charges. Good Girl Donna… You see son, if I haven't taught you anything else, I taught you how to control a bitch!" He yelled in my direction, as the officers told him to keep quiet, and pushed him towards a back door. From that day on, we never saw my father again. He was right, he did teach me something. Men have all the control, all the power, and that real women, knew their place.

- I shall burn only for my sins, but I shall not burn for the sins of my father…-

Chapter 9

Winning in Love

I get by showing off my good looks. I survive by stealing hearts, and destroying what little love you have left within. I am winning because morality I lack. You think you know me, but I will always surprise you in the End.

Luna…. (Terri)

"mmm…oooohhhh….yes…yes…yes! OH YEAH T. I told you I'd beat dat azz…" She got up to do a mocking touchdown dance, after she made her fourth touchdown on the game in the last half hour. "You know you're crazy right? But that's why I love you…I mean like a homie you know." I can't believe I let that slip out of my mouth. I hadn't told her that before. Not that I didn't mean it. But love for her was different than other women. I loved how much fun we could have together, how she got me on a deeper mental level. I loved how we could go from playing video games, to talking about history and philosophy. She was just another part of me, like an extension of who I really am on the inside. She slowed down dancing, and smiled with that amazingly beautiful smile that she has. "Terri, you don't mean that. I know you, you have a girlfriend, and you also have that one chick you been chasing for years. Then aren't you talking about getting serious with the one girl you've been seeing for the last year? I'd just be another name on the list. What we have is better than love. We appreciate each other, we vibe differently that's all. Don't mess this up babe." She said as she gently pushed me in the chest. Damn, although she was young, she still knew exactly what to say to let me know she wasn't tripping being my side piece. She knew that having another woman isn't what I really wanted, but I also didn't want to lose her. I need her in my life, just like I needed all my women. I'm not a cheater, all my relationships are special and different. She was no different than the others. I loved her in her own special way, and our relationship was ours. She continued to mock me by pretending to shake her butt back and forth in my face. I smiled as I walked up behind her. She jumped forward once she felt my erection rub up against her backside. She laughed, then turned around to face me, and we stood there face to face staring each other down. "Well as you can see, I want you now, and I want you later, and I want you to stay in my life as long as possible. No matter what we're doing, or who we happen to do it with, separately! You will always be my girl."

Summer had arrived faster than I expected. Dev and I had officially been broken up for at least three months, and Terri and I had been officially dating for the last two. Things were going just okay with Terri, we had crazy amounts of sexual chemistry, and undeniably loved spending time together; but something in me just didn't allow me to get too close to him. We decided not to get our families involved in what this thing was that we were building until I was ready. I just couldn't see myself explaining why I was bringing a new man to thanksgiving dinner again for the fourth time in six years.

The week had flown by, and I was elated that I had nothing major to do all weekend. This particular Saturday morning instead of waking up next to my new "man", I woke up alone to the sounds of birds chirping outside my window, and my alarm clock going off, reminding me to get moving and meet Tiana at the gym for an early morning workout. I walked to the bathroom with my cell in tow, realizing that I hadn't heard from Terri since Thursday afternoon. At first I was annoyed, but dismissed the thought by convincing myself that it wasn't a big deal. Unlike Dev, Terri traveled for work, and sometimes he would leave for days, and I wouldn't hear from him if he was caught up in a conference or meetings all day. When he left for California Thursday night, he told me that he would call me as soon as things settled down. "It's alright, he's obviously just jet lagged, and busy, not to mention they are three hours behind us." I'm speaking to myself in the mirror as I brush my teeth. Terri and I were good. Things were smooth sailing, and we had no problems to report. I just need to calm down, and not be so paranoid.

The gym was busier than usual, some basketball tournament had men and women flooding the fitness center to either watch on the sidelines, or warm-up while they waited for their match. Tiana and I found the last two treadmills that were side by side, so we quickly snatched them up before anyone noticed they were free. "You okay girl? You seem like something is bothering you. You've been acting stranger than usual." Tiana was very inquisitive, but I was in no mood to express how I was feeling. So I look up from the machine and shrug her comment off, "Who me? Psshht, I'm fine. Just hungry, and a little tired. Haven't been sleeping well." She smiled then jumped in. "I bet you haven't been sleeping well with that fine ass man I saw coming out of your house last week. Girl, whatever he's selling, I'll take two of each!" We both threw our hands up to high-five in agreement. "I know right. He is magically delicious. But no, he's been away on business. I'm just staying up late working on this major project at work. Let me ask you something. When you broke things off with Aaron, and started seeing Dorian, did you feel weird, or uneasy in the beginning of the relationship with Dorian? Maybe like you didn't trust him?" She looked at me and shook her head. "Of course. Aaron slept with god knows how many women while we were together. I didn't think I could trust Dorian for a long time. But Dorian is different. The first few months are gonna be hard girl. Just remember, punish your current man for current things, not for the sins of your previous man. If you feel like something is off, don't investigate it, ask him directly. If he says it's nothing, it's up to you to decipher if his actions line up with his words or not." I wasn't looking at her, but I heard every word, and let them sink in and resonate with me. "My only concern with Terri, is that he spends a lot of time with his mom and family, and sometimes we go days without seeing each other because of his job too. I don't want to be too clingy and lose him. But I also don't want to be a fool either, and potentially find myself in another bad situation." She had increased her speed, but was still able to talk. "You'll figure it out. If he hasn't shown you any negative signs other than working too hard, and taking care of his momma, then you aren't in a bad situation girl. You gotta relax."

When we finished our workout, we grabbed our bags and walked to our cars. "So Luna, we still on for sushi later?" "Girl, do you think I'm gonna walk two and a half miles, lift heavy ass weights, and not eat sushi later? Uhhh No... I will be eating my body weight sashimi and crunch rolls." We laughed so hard I almost fell over. I had plenty of time to spend with my girls, since Terri wouldn't be back in town until Monday anyway.

Dev

"Marina, listen I understand your situation, but if I'm asking you to be here at a certain time, it's because I need you to be here at that time. In the future, if you gonna be late, don't bother coming." I hung up the phone because I didn't need to hear her dumb ass excuses. I'm the one taking all the risk right now, I just need her to do what I'm asking her to do. We had been messing around for that last couple months, and things have been pretty solid. She's actually pretty cool, considering the whole age thing. Other than the age difference, I could see this being a solid jump off option until I meet my Mrs. Right. I've still been meeting other chicks, even went out on a couple dates. Nothing really serious came out of the situations, bitches be expecting too much, and as men we get too little in return. Sherrod and I were just talking the other day about how hoes be wanting dinner, movies, and five and six dates before they given up the ass. "Bruh, if she not fucking and sucking after a burger and fries on the first night, what is we doing?" Sherrod said as we both laughed. "You know, why do chicks think that holding out is going to make us want them more?" I said to him really wondering who told chicks that dumb lie about guys. Sherrod answered me quickly. "I don't know, but it only makes me want to delete their number faster." We both are rolling laughing at this point. When it all comes down to it, bitches need to remember who's the boss in a relationship, or any situation when it comes to men; we run shit, do what you're told and shut your mouths. All of my boys thought this way, so there's no way all of us are wrong. Marina texted me back almost immediately after I hung up.

SMS: M-Sexy: *"Dev, please don't be mad, my brother been keeping a close eye on me this weekend, and my dad said he wanted us to go away and see our family up North. I'll make it up to you Sunday night, or any day next week. Just don't be mad okay?"*

Yeah whatever, I say out loud. Man that was my only guaranteed ass this weekend. Now I have to get into suave mode to see if I can convince another trick to come through tonight. As soon as I was about to press send on a message to a chick named Carina I had met a few times, my mom's picture popped up on my phone. "Hey ma what's up?" "Hey baby, it's been a while since I heard from you, trying to make sure you're doing okay?" I know she's just lonely, since my she lives alone now after Ariyana moved in with one of her friends from college. She never remarried, or dated seriously after all that shit went down with my father. I never got over how mad I was with her for putting up with his shit, and even more upset that she didn't press charges. So I keep my distance, and hardly speak to her. "I'm good, a little busy you know. Is everything okay?" Even though I clearly wasn't busy, I never have a desire to talk to my mom, or any family for that matter. I'm the successful one now, and I hate that my family calls me looking for hand-outs. "Ohh yeah, I'm good, was sick last week, and you know things have been tight since I lost my job at the doctor's office. You know where I was the receptionist. But good news, I've been working at a nursing home, it's okay money. I just hate taking three buses to get there. Well I won't bore you with that stuff. I just wanted to say I love you and miss you, and wish you'd come visit me sometime." I was so busy looking at Carina's ass in a swimsuit picture she had recently posted on her profile page, that I didn't hear what my mother was talking about. "Yeah mom, I'll do that soon okay. Is there anything else?" I said trying to rush her off the phone. "No Dev, that's it. I love you son." "Love you too ma."

An hour after I texted Carina, there she was knocking at my door. She was average looking, but I wasn't worried about what she looked like on the outside, I planned on keeping the lights off the whole time I was handling my business. As she walked in the house, I cut straight to the chase. "Look Carina, I like you, a lot actually; and I've been enjoying us hanging out lately. I asked you over because…" I pause and bite my lip seductively. "Girl, I need to make love to you tonight." She started to blush, that's all I needed to see. Bitches loved when dudes said stuff like make love, instead of saying fucking. Little do y'all know, it's all the same, cause we don't love y'all. She walked over wrapped her arms around my neck and hugged me tight. "Dev that's so sweet. I like you too, you know I've been waiting for you to make your move, so tonight is as good as any I guess." She whispered in my ear, and with that, I took her hand and walked her to my bedroom. Reminder to self, buy Sherrod dinner for his recent bit of advice. "Talk to hoes as if I planned on making them my woman." My dude is getting me hella ass nowadays. The least I can do, is get him a good meal.

Luna

"Hey girl, so how have things been going with Dev?" "Ohh he's right where you want him to be, we've been hooking up on and off for a while now. I think he likes me, but it's not real serious." I smiled into the phone. "Good, good. Ok, fall off from talking to him for a few days, or maybe like a week. Then come back and tell him your pregnant; but only after y'all have sex again. Cool?" She paused, but then agrees to the plan. "Yeah of course, I gotcha! I know what's supposed to happen." I smiled knowing that my plan was coming together perfectly. One dumb bitch, plus one dumb bitch made man, equals one broken heart that will take years to repair. If all goes right, Dev will never hurt another woman again.

- Be careful when you seek vengeance on your fellow man. The coal you hold will burn, and the scar may never heal.-

Chapter 10

Not What I Expected

I am worthy of love, just as worthy as the love I give to you. For if you see into my soul, it is a reflection of all the things I say and Do. I am in need of compassion and intimacy, just like you are in need of food, water, and air. For when you take these things away from me, this life I cannot live, for I cannot bear. Give me what I ask of you, and I promise to give you so much more. For if you deliver just a fraction of love for me, there is no way you can handle the amount I'd give in return.

Dev

"Bruh I've gotten so much pussy lately, I can't even keep count. I promise you, I haven't been happier! Matter of fact, the other night while I was smashing this one hoe, I think I called this bitch by another bitches name. Check this out though, she didn't even get mad. For real bruh, these hoes are so easy it's ridiculous." We all laughed at my theatrics. I was smiling from ear to ear, throwing my hands around, just giving my guys exactly what I knew they wanted to hear. Besides, as much pussy as I've been getting, I know I'm keeping condom companies in business. I had to have spent at least $100 or more on rubbers in the past few weeks. Me, Sherrod, and our homie Marcel were getting breakfast at one of our favorite spots downtown. I told Sherrod I owed him a good meal for putting me onto some of his best hookup apps, and teaching me some of his tricks that made getting pussy easier than ever. Marcel, who claims to be this goody boy Christian, always telling us to calm down, and treat women better. I always tell him the same thing; when I find a hoe who deserves it, she'll get it. Most of these bitches are the same. They all are trying to get something out of a man. Whether it's meals, money, gifts, a ring, whatever. We have to put in the heavy lifting, and they reap all the fucking benefits. It's time for us to get what we want; Pussy. That's where I'm at right now. Fuck these stupid ass tricks, and thanks to Luna, I have no desire to fall in love again, any time soon.

The server dropped off a few more glasses juice to our table, and walked away before we continued our conversation. "Man it's all fun and games now, but what happens when we're old and grey? What happens when one day you have a daughter you have to look in the face knowing you've treated women horribly for years? What happens when the woman you want and love, doesn't want or love you? Karma is real dog, and one day it comes back when you least expect it." Marcel says seriously, as we looked at him, paused and looked around, before both Sherrod and I laughed and continued to shove mounds of pancakes and bacon into our mouths. "Man shut up." Said Sherrod, swatting at the air as if to dismiss everything that he was saying. "First of all, we're still in our twenties, we have plenty of time to settle down. Second, you act like we're scamming these hoes. They know what they signed up for when it comes to me at least. I'm not promising love, friendship, or a future. Hell I don't even promise these tricks a warm meal in the morning. I'm giving the D&D. Dick and door my friend. Giving her the dick, and showing her the door." Sherrod reached out to give me a handshake. I hesitated at first, cause it felt a little wrong, but then again I had to agree with him; I'm not making promises anymore. I don't promise these girls anything, and that's what I loved about it most. Luna suckered me in with this shit about her wanting a long term relationship, and how she deserved love and respect. Okay, I fell for it for a little while. She never asked what I felt I deserved. Like sex on call any time I wanted it. Nonetheless, my guys had the right idea, don't love these hoes. If bitches were really smarter, they wouldn't give it up so easily, and get played the way they do. Then again, I'm glad these hoes are dumb, I need more stupid tricks in my life. Speaking of dummies, one was calling right now. I picked up the phone after seeing M-Sexy on the screen. I didn't even say hello, I just cut straight to the chase. "Hey, what's up? You coming through later?" Marina responded in her sweet innocent voice, "Yeah, I was able to get free from my dad and brother. So you know I'm coming. I miss you baby." "Yeah I know you do. Well don't wear no panties, just a skirt for easy access, hahaha! I'll see you later aight?" I hung up without saying goodbye. "And that's how you do it fellas. Just like that, I got plans for later tonight." Sherrod looked directly at Marcel, and replied. "That's how it goes, keep it short, no promises, and keep these hoes coming back for more."

Luna

Miles Davis played quietly in the background as I laid on my couch reading a book, waiting for Apryl to come over. I hadn't kept in touch with her recently, and that night she was drunk still plagued my thoughts whether she knew it or not. I felt so horrible for trying to get rid of her, just so that I could get some. Even though she said it was no big deal, I still kept trying to make it up to her. Since Terri was away on business in Tennessee this weekend, I told her to come by and we would have a girl's day, just the two of us.

My phone started to vibrate on the coffee table right next to me. I reached over to see her text that she was about fifteen minutes away. I decided to get up to take out a few glasses for wine, and turn the oven on. I planned on making my famous stuffed shells, with sautéed veggies. I made it for Terri last month, and he claimed to have loved it. The thought of him made me smile. Actually now that I think of it, that was the one person I hadn't heard from all day today. This was becoming a bad habit for him. Every time he went away for his business, he would go days without speaking to me, only to come back and tell me he was so busy, or he lost track of time. I trusted him, and I didn't want to be a nag, but this shit is getting pretty old. Point is, I was starting to be over this whole situationship we were in. I was going to give him one last chance. But instead of waiting for him to reach out to me, I decided to be proactive and reach out to him.

SMS: *Hey baby, I miss you. Just wanted to say hello, Hope to see you this week if you have time. Love -Lu-*

(Knock Knock Knock) I guess I lost track of time, or either Apryl was hella fast. I peeked through my kitchen window to see who was outside before rushing to the front door. As I expected, Apryl was standing there looking anxious to get inside, as I'm sure it was blazing hot. "Well, Hey girl Hey! I

65

been missing my little cousin." I said as I embraced her, and pulled her into the cool air that flowed throughout the townhouse. We laughed for a second as we began making taunting jokes at one another. I walked into the kitchen to pour her a huge glass of wine, and asked how she had been doing lately. "No time to waste, fill me in, and let's get this party started." I say then hand her the glass and prepare to toast.

Two Hours Later..

I still hadn't gotten a response from Terri. I was finally giving up on hearing back from him today. Although I knew he was going away on business, it's still Saturday night, and I'm sure he had at least five minutes to check his phone and respond to me. "You know what, I'm not letting this man ruin my good mood, and quality time with my cousin." I say to myself, as I watch Apryl dancing to old TLC songs playing on through my speakers in the room. I head to the kitchen to pour another glass of wine, and ask if she wanted to watch a movie. "Yeah girl, that sounds cool. So I creep yeah just keep it on the down low… uh uh uh." She sang as I laughed at her bad dancing while I walked away.

Why was I so engulfed in wanting to know what was going on with Terri, and why wasn't he responding to me? Do I really care about him that much? Oh god, am I in love? I didn't notice Apryl picking up my vibrating phone, because I was too busy trying to shake off the thoughts of being in love with Terri when I never wanted to be. "Hey cuz, some very handsome guy is calling you named T. Who's T?" I started to rush back into the living room, but stopped dead in my tracks, because I knew I looked thirsty. Finally he calls back I thought as I snatched the phone. I was so pissed that it took him so long to get back to me, so now I wanted him to think I was busy. "I'm not gonna answer it." I tell her dryly. Right after the missed call, he sends a text.

SMS: T: *Baby I'm so sorry I've been so busy this weekend. But I promise to make it up to you Monday night. How bout I come by and cook you dinner? Let me know if you're free. Luv u… T*

She snatched my phone back from my hand and read my text message a loud. "Ohhh… T huh? That T must stand for Tasty, or Terrific, or TEARIN UP that nasty kitty!" She stuck out her tongue, made a cat sound, and we both laughed as if on cue. As soon as I gained my composure, I raised my hand in the air to stop her, then added a sigh of frustration. "Please… He's not tearing up anything around here no time soon. I'm so pissed right now. Gawd! I mean, why do men play these games ya know? Why do I have to feel like I'm on some kind of list with him; hell with men in general? Why is it that…. he can go missing for days now, and if I'm not available and on call for him, he's all in his feelings? I just want it to be easier cuz." I sighed, almost feeling like I wanted to cry, thinking about Dev, and Terri both at the same damn time. "I just want love to be the way I imagine it in my head." I came back to the couch holding the remote, completely forgetting the wine glasses. I collapsed on the sofa as if I lost all control of my legs. She shuffled over and sat near me, then began to rub my head gently. "Listen cousin, you're not the only one. Love is only complicated because we make it that way. I don't care about finding a love like the one you believe in your head right now. It's like this, if a man isn't making me happy, or giving me what I want; then what the fuck is he good for? Take my half-sister Leah for instance. She barely sees this guy she's been dating for the last three years, but he recently asked her to marry him, and this dummy said YES! I don't even think my father knows him that well. Now don't get me wrong he's fine, helps pay her bills, and seems to really like her, but he's always claiming to be taking care of his mom, traveling for work, and not to mention, he has family in New York so he's always claiming to be flying out to spend time with them. But… he's the man she wants, and they make it work. Like right now, he took her down south for some couples retreat this weekend, in like Louisiana or Tennessee somewhere. Point is, if you like this guy, you have to decide to make it work with Mr. T." She said then giggled at the name Mr. T. I laid there, thinking about how similar Leah's man was to Terri. I didn't try to hard to put things together, I actually wished I could just ask them how they make their relationship work. Just before I could start to ask Apryl a question about her sisters man, she continued. "Speaking of which Leah's man looks a lot like the picture of Mr.

67

sexy chocolate in your phone. Then again, all dark-skinned men all look-alike to me. I think his name is Thomas, Terrence, Toni…" I interject, "Terri?" She looked at me with excitement and continued "Yeah, that's right. Terri. Real nice guy too. I met him once, he is fine as hell cuz! They been going strong for like three years. He has friends out here I think, so I know he spends a lot of time down this way. But he's been moving in with her these last few weeks. Or at least he has been bringing shit over to her house is what she told me." She rambled on and on, not paying attention to the fact that I laid there completely paralyzed from the neck down. Without any conscious thought, I got up and ran to the bathroom and began throwing up all of food and wine I'd ingested for the last couple of hours. Apryl ran in after a few minutes of listening to me heaving, I lifted my head up from the porcelain bowl and whisper. "He's a fucking cheater!"

-     I played... I won... I'm guilty of fraud....-

Chapter 11

Liars and Losers

You Lied…. You told me you were in love. You told me I was the one. You told me that no one else could compare. But you left me standing, and I was the only one there. You lied. You didn't mean to keep me. You didn't mean to make this last. You Gave me just a piece of you. But now you're gone, and love is in my past…

Dev

"Damn girl, you keep surprising me! Just when I think we've done it all, you do something to take me to another level. You so nasty." I said as I grabbed her face and kissed her deeply in the mouth. "If you keep doing stuff like this, I may just have to keep you around long-term. Maybe until you're old enough to be my girl publicly." She smiled softly, and nibbled on her top lip as she looked away. Marina and I were in a good place. I was getting ass when I wanted, I didn't have to take her out anywhere, not like I really could; but basically all I had to do was call her, and just like a delivery pizza, thirty minutes later I was being served. I was starting to feel bad about what I was doing to her. She was young and dumb, and was willing to do anything, I mean ANYTHING I wanted to do sexually. But then again, another part of me felt justified. She knew what we were doing, and until she says she doesn't want to do this anymore, I'm gonna keep get whatever I can, while I can. She walked across the room picking up her clothes and jewelry that were thrown just about everywhere. Things typically escalate quickly when it comes to sex between her and I. A part of me still felt like a creep whenever she came by the house. I always felt like I was one episode away from being on To Catch a Predator. I looked out the door to see if she was followed, always deleted our texts and cleared my history daily, and limited what I said to her in case anyone was by chance looking through her phone. I didn't want any problems, and so far, I didn't have them. To keep it real, if she were older, and a little wiser, she would definitely be wifey material. However for now, she's just a piece of ass; nothing more, probably less.

Finally, when she was fully put together, and ready to leave, I told her to wait that I needed to talk to her. At the last second Sherrod left to go be with his dad for the week, I wanted to do something different with her. Instead of just showing her out the door after sex, I decided to order some chinese food, start a movie, and let her stay a while so we could kick it. I held her hand gently in the palm of mine and looked deeply into her eyes. "So can you chill with me for a little bit? I don't want you to feel like I'm always trying to put you out after, ya know. You're more important to me than that." I started slightly swinging her hand back and forth like we were playing a game. "Yeah D, that would be nice. Thank you!" Her face lit up as if I said I was gonna buy her a new car. Damn, it is too easy to impress this hoe, I thought. I walked down the stairs toward the kitchen to get a menu, and yelled up to her to tell me what she wanted to eat. "Ohh, I just want chicken fried rice and an egg roll please." Marina said as she went back into my room to use the bathroom. Once she had finished, I heard her making her way to the living room to sit on the couch. I came in to join her, after placing our order, and grabbing us both some chips and drinks to get started with until our food arrived. I handed her a glass of soda, then sat next to her on the couch. I wrapped my arms around her, as she settled her head into the center of my chest. It felt good, really good to be honest. To feel genuine affection from a woman again. I hadn't felt like this since Luna, well it wasn't quite the same as Luna, but similar enough to remind me of what it felt like for someone to want you, to need you as a man. I looked down at the top of her head, and for a brief moment started to say to her, damn this feels fucking amazing. But I didn't want to give her any sense of hope for a relationship.

We finished our food, just as the movie was coming to an end. It's wasn't as late as I thought, so I put on a comedy special just for laughs. At first we were both laughing, but after a while I must've dozed off, because I didn't hear any laughter for a long while. I woke up as the screen had returned to the menu. I began to stretch a little since my whole body was stiff from sitting in the same position for so long. Without even checking to see if Marina was awake, I started to speak. "Man tonight was fun! Don't you think?" Apparently I am talking to myself. I noticed that Marina was drooling on my shirt, looking so sweet and peaceful. I had to bring myself back to reality, cause I was starting to feel things for her, that I should be feeling, like concern. (SHE IS A MINOR, SHE IS A HOE, SHE IS NOT YOUR GIRL BRUH). "Yo Marina, yo… Yo you gotta go, it's getting late." I said as I shook her gently. She leaned back, stretched both hands in the air, and wiped the drool from her mouth, and sleep from her eyes. "Yeah, wow! It is getting late. Thanks Dev, I'm gonna head out. Thank you for tonight D, even though I know I'm not your girl, this made me feel really special." She leaned in to kiss me passionately, and at the same time breathed in my air. I pushed her away, and held her shoulders before speaking. "Listen. You know what this is. We not doing that emotional shit." She turned away from me, stood up from the sofa visably disappointed, she grabbed the rest of her things and walked to the door. "SHIT" I sat there for a second feeling like a total ass hole, but I knew I had to keep things clear, and be honest. I rushed behind her, and yelled for her to wait up so that I could let her out. As we stood at the door, I felt compelled to tell her the truth. "Marina, you are still special to me. But you know we can't be serious, for SO many reasons. Not to mention that I'm not looking for a girlfriend. I'm just trying to fuck. So this just can't be anything more than what we are." She turned the left corner of mouth up into a bitter scowl. "Marina baby girl, don't do this, you know what we agreed on, and you know I'm gonna keep you around. That's why I let you stay so late tonight. Come on?" I said until she softened up a little. She seemed to smirk just slightly, then began to respond. "That's cool. But just so you know, I left you a gift on your bed; a pregnancy test. Ohh and by the way.. It's yours. Yup…. I'm PREGNANT!"

Luna

I couldn't stop crying, I was sitting on the floor in my downstairs bathroom, still dry heaving into my toilet bowl. "He's a fucking liar, Ohhhh GAWD! How could I be so stupid? Why me again?" Hardly able to stream together a coherent sentence, I started feeling what was left in my stomach coming up

71

again. I rushed back to the toilet bowl, tears streaming down my face, stomach cramping, but nothing came out. Apryl was so confused as to what was going on, and who I was talking about. She just held my hair back, and rubbed my shoulders. "Baby who's a liar? Do you want me to get you some ginger ale, or soda water? Calm down, and tell me what you need." I finally started to pull myself together, and sat up straight. "No, I'm good." I take a deep breath, and exhale. "I'm just gonna fucking ruin his whole damn life. Dev…. That's who I'm mad at." I look around hoping she didn't notice that I was clearly lying. I didn't want her to tell her sister that her man was possibly my man too. Not until I had a plan in place. So I just went with the whole I'm drunk and still hurting over the breakup with Dev thing, until I could appropriately fill Apryl in. "Well, that's fine hun, to be mad at Dev still. He's an asshole, let me help you up okay?" She said with concern in her voice as she helped me over to the couch, and went into the kitchen to get me some water and crackers. She turned on a movie as I laid in her lap while she stroked my head. All the while I laid there, my mind I was plotting on just how I could expose Terri for being the piece of trash I now suspect him to be. There is no way all of this was a coincidence. He's in the south, not answering my calls, while her sister is gone with a guy named Terri who looks like my man. Really, bitch please. I know my cousin wasn't bright enough to put two and two together, but I knew better, and I knew just what to do to fix his lying cheating ass. Terri and Dev picked the wrong bitch to play with.

Apryl fell asleep on the couch shortly after the movie started, and the natural light from the moon gleamed through the living room window, and illuminated the space. So many thoughts were racing through my mind. When did this shit start, how long has it been going on, or more important, why didn't I notice that I was dating a soon to be married man? No answers could come to mind, simply because I was also so consumed with being ready to take Terri off the face of the Earth. I'm done being the punchline of these guys jokes. Done being the good girl. I already know I'm fucking up Dev's life, but now I have to destroy Terri, COMPLETELY. I picked up my phone, and began to draft a text.

SMS: *Hey babe, I apologize for the late response. My cousin stopped by and we were in the midst of a girls night. Anywho, Monday sounds great, can't wait to see you! Ohh yeah, did I tell you that I miss you so much, and I wanna see your face like right now… can you video chat with me in the morning before you take off to head home? You know, show me what I'm missing… wink wink… Luv Lu…*

"Yeah Terri, I can't wait to see you Monday." I say in a whisper. Monday will be the beginning of the end for him. "I'm done being fucking played with."

Dev

"Da Fuck you mean pregnant?" I yelled at Marina as I snatched her back in the door, and pulled her aggressively through the house and up the stairs towards my bedroom. She wiggled and fought me each step of the way. I swing open my door to find an envelope on my bed with a pregnancy test stick laying underneath it. "Are you serious Marina? Who the fuck does this? What kind of games are you on?" I'm screaming the entire time, never even bothering to open the stupid ass card she left. She finally is free of my grasp, and is throwing her hands all in my face, as she theatrically tells me about this so-called pregnancy. "Game? What do you mean? We've had sex how many times D? And not all of those times did you use protection, or were you careful. I stopped taking my birth control over a month ago, and I told you that the first time we messed around, that I was getting off the pill. And just because you think I'm a hoe, doesn't mean I really am. I've only been fucking you, so now it is what it is…. Guess we're having a baby. Unless you want me to…. Ya know?" She said putting her head down as if she were too afraid to use the word abortion. Well if she didn't want to say it, I did. "Uhhh Yeah bitch, you need to kill it. You don't need a baby, and I definitely don't want no kids with a damn child. Bitch you ain't even outta high school yet. Get yo life right!" I yelled as I began to look up clinics in the area on my cell phone. She stepped back towards the door looking as if she needed to brace herself. She clearly was beyond angry, but shit I was too. I wasn't ready to be no daddy, nor was I built for jail. She started to speak in a low growl. "Oh yeah, how do you think it's gonna go over when I have to tell the clinic I got pregnant by a grown ass man? Or how about my father? Or hell my brother? You think my brother is gonna be cool with me fucking you, then you getting me pregnant, and forcing me to get rid of my child? How about I call him right now to ask him to come get me from my baby daddy's house?" She reached for her purse to get to her phone. I jumped across the bed to knock the phone to the floor. "Aight AIGHT… Be cool. We will figure this out. Shit. Let me think….." I was freaking out, and this shit was beyond surreal. I didn't know what I was about to say, I just began to give her instructions. "Okay listen, go home tonight. Let's get our heads straight, and uhh, see if your dad will be cool with you staying the night with your friend in two days. Just make some shit up. We are gonna figure this out Marina, I apologize for yelling." I begin to walk towards her with my arms open wide. "Just go home and get some rest, I'll call you tomorrow." I hugged her tightly, exhaled, then pulled back to kiss her gently on the forehead. She took a deep breath, and sighed with relief. "Thank you D. I'm scared you know. I just want to do the right thing." She said through tears that were starting to fall down her face. "I know, I'm take of you." I say as I wipe her tears away. Finally I walked her to her car, hugged her again, and kissed her goodnight. I waited to watch her drive off, then walked to over to my car to head to the store. "I guess I gotta take control of the situation myself."

Luna

"I am beautiful, I am desired, I am wanted, I am strong, I am confident, I am….." Knock, knock, knock. The knock at the door distracts me from focusing on my reflection in my bedroom mirror. That must be Terri outside. Returning my focus once again to the mirror, I say my last I am statement before I walk out of the room. "I am… going to fuck this mutha fucka up, for playing me." I smiled sweetly, then made my way towards the stairs, and down to face the man of the hour. It was always important for me to say my I am statements before leaving the house, or before going on a date. They constantly remind me that I am all that I say I am; But what I am not, is a damn fool. I couldn't believe that Terri would do this to me, after all we've been to each other. Not to mention the fact that we've known each other for

YEARS! This is the shit that a guy does to a girl he just met, or to a girl he's been dating for a little while, but never really cared about. He and I were never that serious for him to lie to me like this. Hell, if he had only told me the truth from day one, I may have still let him hit it, cause I was just trying to get over Dev, and I never really wanted to fall in love. But no, he had to say all this stuff about keeping me in his life, and building a relationship. Bullshit! Now that I know that he's no different from any of the others, now I know how to treat him like the others, I thought.

At the base of the stairs was a mirror hanging from the wall. I glance at myself to fix my hair and make up, and take a deep breath once more before I go to open the door. I slowly strut across the living room, trying to plaster a fake I'm so glad to see you smile on my face. "Hi T! I missed you so much." I say innocently as I reached out to hug him, as I let my breast jiggle intentionally in my top. I didn't wear a bra with my crop top on purpose, and the white shirt was just thin enough that he could see my nipples without seeing my bare chest. My tight grey pencil skirt hugged my hips so close that it looked like a second layer of skin. His mouth dropped open as he took all of me in with a quick once over. "Umm…. Hey Lu! You look.. I mean… Your outfit is… What were we doing? Girl I can't even find words to express how fine you look right now. Just DAYYYYUUUMMM" He stumbled over each letter that came out of his mouth. I giggled like an innocent school girl as he tried to continue. "Luna, were we going somewhere, I thought I was just gonna cook some dinner, and we were gonna chill?" He looked stunned, and that's exactly how I wanted him to look and feel, stunned, confused and not sure what to think. "Of course we are just staying in. I just know you've been working so hard lately, and been gone a lot, so I just wanted to show you what you've been missing." I needed him completely distracted for what was going to transpire tonight.

As he cooked dinner I told him I had a surprise for him in my car. I knew he wasn't paying attention so I swiped his keys at the same time I grabbed mine. I went outside where I quickly did what I needed to do to get his "surprise together". I came back into the house where he was plating our food and I sat down to eat. He lit a single candle at the table, poured a couple of glasses of my favorite red wine, and we began to eat. After a few minutes he began to speak. "You know Luna I'm really glad that you're in my life. You are a really amazing woman, and the fact that you're entertaining a man like me... you know." He paused as if he were really fucking sincere. Then he started again. "Luna, I just feel like I'm falling in love with you." I could barely hold back my sarcastic eye roll. "Really T? In Love? It's so soon. I think you should really think about your feelings before professing something so serious like love to me." He cut me off. "No I mean it. You see.... Wait, did you hear that?" Terri paused after we both heard yelling coming from outside. Right on time, I thought. We both turned to look towards the living room door, as we both recognized what sounded like Apryl screaming outside the door. Except instead of saying my name this time, she was screaming his name. I calmly stand up and shake my head in disappointment. "What the hell is going on? Excuse me Terri, I'll go handle this." I rush across the house to open the door, and in walks Apryl and her half-sister Leah. Apryl was holding her phone as if she were recording, all while still yelling his name. "Terri... Terri! I hope y'all have enough food for two more people, you lying piece of shit." Terri stood up from the table in complete shock. "What the fuck is this?" Terri asked. I turned to him and smiled. "Ohh this, I guess it looks like a ghetto version of cheaters. You're busted."

- Game, set, use the match to set that cheaters shit on fire.-

Chapter 12....

Truth comes in phases

There comes a time in life when you just have to be honest. You have to look yourself in the mirror and say. I messed up... I apologize. There comes a moment when you can no longer be the man or woman you've always been. You have to be better. Better for you, better for me, better for all of us.... Now is that time!

Dev

I'm sure the night air should have felt colder to me, but I was so focused on getting shit done, that I didn't even notice. I let the windows down in my ride, and opened the sun roof, as I cruised through the city trying to figure out what I could do to get this situation under control. Marina did some foul shit tonight. Leaving a card on my bed that said congratulations you're gonna be a dad. Congratulations? Yeah right. More like surprise bitch, your life is all the way over. This means jail, I lose my job, fuck, I might even have to register as a sex offender. There were so many thoughts running through my mind, that I almost ran a red light by not paying attention. I have to fix this, like right now. Bringing my attention back to the current moment, I see a drug store up the block, and decide to pull over and call Sherrod for advice.

"Yo bro what's good?" Sherrod said calmly as if he were just chilling alone, but I could clearly hear a chicks voice in the background. "Oh you busy bruh? I can hit you up later if you're in the middle of something." I say casually, but really hoping he curves this bitch, whoever she is, long enough to answer some of my questions. "Nah you good. Let me go somewhere quiet.... Yo Ash I'll be right back, aight?" Sherrod said as he walked out the room, and headed somewhere that was a lot quieter. He tells me to go ahead, as I begin to give him a version of events that doesn't incriminate me. "So basically, I've been smashing this hoe for a few weeks, maybe a month or more, and she tells me tonight that she's pregnant." I say casually hoping he doesn't ask who the chick is. I pause for a second, then continue. "What it all comes down to is that she's not quite sure she wants to keep the baby. You know me, I'm not trying to be no family man with no hoe. I'm going to be a father to my kids with my wife, not with some chick that I'm just breaking off. So what can she take to ya know, get rid of it?" He let out a deep exhale into the mouthpiece of the phone, as if it were happening to him. "Man D, can't you just take her to the clinic? You might have to take a L on that bread, and just get it taken care of that way." I sighed too. "Bruh, she ain't trying to go to a clinic. Something about her dad being a popular doctor around here or some shit, she don't want it to get back to him. Basically she trying to do this the old fashion, like the homemade way to get rid of this shit." He obviously wasn't picking up what I was trying to express. Why couldn't he just tell me what I needed to do, to be rid of this baby situation, and fall back from this girl forever. Sherrod paused for a second then continued. "Listen bro, I got two plan B pills in my room, in the top drawer of my dresser. Go buy another one tonight, cause you need three. I'm gonna text you a list of a few herbs you need, to basically soak them shits over night. Add it to any drink she likes; tell her be easy, she won't even taste them, because they don't have a taste. Then tell her that after she drinks the herb mix, to take all three morning after pills in a twenty-four hour period. One in the morning, lunch, and at night, and that's it. I had a chick put me onto this process about a year ago. Pretty much she's gonna cramp for a day or two, but after that, the baby will be just a memory." I found a ripped piece of paper, and a pen in the glove box of my car so that I could write down what he was saying quick. I didn't want to forget a single detail, and have to call him back again. "Bro! You have no idea how grateful I am." I say with a huge smile on my face, ready to start looking up stores where I can buy this shit. Sherrod didn't sound as happy as I was.

"Yo, next time bruh, you gotta be more careful. For real, a baby is the least of your worries now a days. Not to mention, shorty might not have been so honest about being willing to get rid of it. This really turned out in your favor." Sherrod said more like a big brother, and less like the man I know who used to be advising me on getting more pussy. I listened, but rolled my eyes, cause really I was just more concerned with resolving this situation. Fuck what he's trying to school me on. I need this shit to be handled quick. However, I wasn't going to say that to his face. "You right bruh. But check it. I'm about to run in this store, to get this stuff, so you get back to your lil shorty, and I'll get back to you later."

Luna

Terri stood back, then paced the floor for a second thinking of what he would say. Then he stopped and exposed a flirtatious smile. "Nah, I'm not busted. Maybe my truth was exposed in a way that wasn't ideal. But I can't be busted. I didn't cheat on either one of you." We all stood there looking at his ass confused, and in disbelief. How arrogant of this asshole to act as if he's not in the wrong here. Before I could even begin give him some quality words, Leah jumped in. "What the fuck Terri? You didn't cheat on me? Are you serious? So when I get a call from my sister with her cousin on the line, talking about she thinks my man is her man too, that's not you cheating? The fact that you two have been sleeping together for months, also doesn't count as cheating? You just asked me to marry you a few weeks ago, and started to move your stuff in like we're all good. So please, tell me how you're not cheating on both of us?" She stood by the door with a look in her eye that said, if he says the wrong thing, she may actually kill him. Apryl all the while was rolling her neck, and waving her finger back and forth, still holding up her phone recording the entire thing on a live social media stream. "First, can she please shut that shit off. We're all adults here and I want my chance to explain." Apryl put her phone down, but I noticed that it was never turned off. Which if shit got worse, may be a good thing for evidence sake. He thanked her sarcastically then continued. "First of all, I do love you Leah!" "BULLSHIT!!!!" I screamed. "Luna, come on. Damn. I do love her, she is an amazing woman and I would be happy to make her my wife. However Luna I love you too. We've had an amazing time together, and I could see myself spending more time with you. I didn't know how to tell either of you but, I believe in polygamy." We all looked at each other confused. He went on. "If you wanted to go be with someone else Lu, and still wanted to come back to me occasionally, that's fine too. I don't think love, or physical connections should be… suffocated." I couldn't believe my ears, and by the look on their faces, neither could any of the other woman in the room. Polygamy, did this dude really just try to play that card? He kept talking for a second, although through my rage I couldn't clearly make out what he was saying. Something about how he sees himself in individual relationships with each of us, one never overlapping the other, some dumb shit. I couldn't hold back anymore. "Terri shut up. You sound ridiculous. And you know what, I don't believe in that polygamy shit. How about this. I believe if you were sleeping with multiple people, and felt the way you did about each of them, you should have given us all the chance to decide if we wanted to be apart of your sick ass games or not. This shit you're talking about now, is a lie Terri. Plain and simple." Just like that, I broke open the flood gates, and we all started screaming at him. Leah and I had so much to get off our chest, and we were for damn sure going to make sure he got all of it. Every few seconds we could hear him trying to give some half ass explanation, but we never let him have control of the conversation again. Finally he held up his hands and said. "Alright, alright. I get it! Y'all ain't with this shit, so I'll leave. I'm not gonna keep standing here looking like I did something wrong, when I told y'all what I believe. I never made any of my women feel like they weren't number one when they're with me. Both of you felt special whenever we were together, so I don't even know why you're mad. Just give me my keys, and I'll be out." He said exasperated over the entire ordeal. I threw his keys at him as hard as I could, hitting him in the chest then they fell to the floor. Then I turned and walked over to my couch to grab a box that had a bright red bow on top. We couldn't let him go without a goodbye gift. "Oh wait. We don't want you to leave without giving you your gift." I say with a sarcastic smile. "Why don't you open it now Terri? We think it'll be more special, and important, for you to do it now, rather than walk out and open it later without us." Leah says equally sarcastic and cold. He shook his head, let out a loud sigh, then proceeded to open the large box. "WHHHHAATTT! Ohhhh shit!" He yelled as he pulled out both side-view mirrors from his car, the rear-view mirror, Leah's engagement ring, a piece of paper that said "one free coupon to go fuck yourself", and a receipt for 2 buckets of chitterlings. He left the box there and rushed out the door to see what had been done to his car. We all ran behind him, me grabbing the box, and Apryl with her phone in full camera-woman stance still rolling on the live stream. We all watched him scream in disbelief as he started breaking down next to his car once beautiful new car. All over his 2017 black S-Class Mercedes, was sprayed LIAR, CHEATER, DICK, WHORE in silver sparkling spray paint. His sunroof was wide open, and the night air was wafting the awful stench of dirty chitterlings, which were poured all over his front and back seats. We all stood back far enough to watch him break down. We continued to laugh at him, as he was trying to take in all the damage we had done. I threw his box at him as I yelled in his direction. "We figured since you ain't shit, you wouldn't mind riding home in it! Bon voyage bitch." With that, we all turned around, and walked back to my apartment as we heard Terri pull off and drive away.

Still laughing, from the look on Terri's face when he saw the damage we had done, we closed the door to my house, and began the process of trying to figure out what to do next. I walked over to the sink in the kitchen, and rinse out a few glasses to pour the ladies some wine. I hear Apryl talking to someone, but it wasn't her sister. I stood by the entrance to the living room and watched as reality sat in for Leah, and she began to weep. Apryl and I went over to wrap our arms around her, and remind her that everything would be alright. I sighed out loud truly knowing how she felt, and wishing I could take her pain away. I knew she would have to eventually talk to Terri again, since he had things at her house, but I also knew she would have to come to grips with how she wanted to move forward with their relationship on her own. Their break up, if she goes through with it at all, will be losing a potential husband; not like me just losing a piece of ass. So this journey for her, was going to be far more difficult than I could imagine. I had no kind words to describe Terri, and I didn't know what to say to her about losing her man. All I could add was a little humor to a sad situation. "Well, Leah think of it this way. Now you know who he is, and what he's about. He's riding home smelling ten tons of shit, and in about fifteen minutes, he's going to probably shit on himself." She looked up at me confused. So I continued. "I served him a glass of wine that I let 8 senna leaves soak in for two hours. The leaves are a natural laxative. His bowels will be flowing like Niagra falls any minute now." We all busted out laughing all over again. Hey, what can I say, I couldn't let him go without one more gut punch.

Dev

"Herbs soaked for the last 24 hours, mixed with pink mascato... Check. Crushed up pills... Check. Pasta sauce almost ready... Check. Bout to be done with crazy ass Marina... Double check." I say aloud, as I'm prepping for dinner with Marina tonight. Drugging someone is not my forte, however, I'm also not willing to be a baby daddy to some dumb ass minor, who thinks she's about to ruin my life over catching feelings. "You got this handled D. You got this handled. One more night with this hoe, and it's all over." I turn around when I hear taps on the door, and know that Marina was finally here. I was ready to get this shit over with. Time was of the essence, and I wasn't willing to waste another minute.

Vanilla scented candles filled the air in the room. I made sure her wine was chilled, turned up the smooth jazz playing in the background, and answered the door in full suave mode. "Hey my beautiful lady carrying my baby." I said with a goofy grin on my face, as I wrapped my arms around her and pulled her into the house. She smiled from ear to ear, exposing all of her teeth, and giggling like a little school girl. "I've missed you these last couple of days. I'm glad you were able to convince your dad to let you stay out tonight so that you could spend time with me. Does anyone know you're here?" I tried to ask nonchalantly, sliding it into the conversation as naturally as I could. She backed away and shook her head slowly. "Nah, I told my friends I was with my granny, and told my dad I was at my cousins house on my moms side. So it's just me and you, with no interruptions." She smiled again looking so sexy, and yet so innocent. Dressed in a two piece form fitted jogging suit, that lifted just above her belly. As usual she looks amazing. Nonetheless I have to focus. Tonight was not the night to be falling for any sympathy shit. I had a job to do, so that this could all be behind me. I walk her to the table and pull out a chair for her to sit down. I stand behind her and start to speak. "I know all of this is crazy, and it took me a day or two to really get on board, but I'm with it now. We just need to discuss the details, and decide how we are going to deal with this. You know, the age thing is going to be a big problem cause we still can't be public with our situation." She nodded her head in agreement, and started to speak. "Well to be honest Dev, I...." I stopped her and jumped back in before she could finish. "Listen, let me just take care of you tonight. I know you're preggors now, and you shouldn't drink, but I figured we should celebrate. I looked up online that you can have at least one glass of wine a day, so I got the Mascato you said you like. You know the pink one. I have it chilling in the kitchen. You think you can keep it down?" I asked making the vomit gesture with my hand to my mouth. We both laughed as I walked away. I pour some wine into a glass and add a little ginger soda, just in case it has a smell or taste from the herbs. I pour myself a double shot of whiskey, say a quick prayer under my breath and walk back to the table. "Let's toast to…new adventures, new families, and new days ahead." I say as we touch glasses, then I watch her take a deep sip. Relieved that she seemed to ignore the taste of the herbs, I knew I was one step closer to freedom. I leaned in to kiss her forehead, then walk back to the kitchen to prepare her a special plate. "I made some chicken alfredo, the kind with the green sauce stuff you said you wanted." I yell in her direction from the kitchen. I heard her snickering. "You mean pesto goofy?" She yelled back at me. "I hope you didn't mess it up. Since you've never really made it before, I don't know what to expect." She said sarcastically. I added my own sarcasm quietly under my breath, as I sprinkled the 3 crushed morning after pills over her noodles, before adding extra sauce. "Yeah, well bitch, I expect you to have a stomach ache tomorrow." I mixed the pasta up a little, making sure there were no traces of the pills anywhere to be seen.

"Here you go beautiful." I say as I set the plate in front of her on the table. "I see you enjoyed that wine, do you want some more?" I saw that her glass was already empty. "Oh, no I shouldn't. I don't want anything to happen to the baby." She said grabbing her belly, that was still obviously firm and flat. I shook my head as if to dismiss the thought. "You'll be fine. I mixed some ginger soda in it, so technically you could have just a little more." I took her glass back to the kitchen and filled it up again. When I got back to the table, I saw her mixing the pasta around her plate, as she started to taste the food. Please God, don't let her taste the pills. I say inside. "Not bad." She said with a smirk, as she shoveled fork-full after fork-full into her mouth. With every minute, I'm getting one step closer to my goal, and now I felt calm enough to let my guard down. As the night pressed on, Marina and I started to really have a good time. We talked and laughed for what felt like forever. I was glad that she drank the wine, and ate every piece of pasta on her plate. I know she planned on staying here tonight, then go home in the morning. I was hoping to tear that ass up one last time, send her on her way in the morning, and in a few days, wait for her to call me to tell me the horrible news. I would act broken hearted, but say it's for the best. I had it all planned out.

"Oh man. I'm glad you came around D. I was worried at firsssthhhh.. You maybe... not... hap. Ready. For baby. Yeah?" Marina was swaying back and forth, and started sounding like she was beyond drunk. I hope none of this shit can really hurt her I thought. I just need this baby gone, not an attempted murder charge. "You ok Marina? You don't look so good." I asked with concern while she was still sitting straight up at the table. Although she nodded yes, it was evident that she wasn't okay. Next thing I know, she grabbed her head and started to slide down in the chair. "Ohh, Dev... Can I... go.. lay... in...bed?" Her words were choppy and slurred. I helped stand her up from the table, and took her to the couch, with a glass of water. I noticed her eyes rolling up and down in her head, and now she was starting to look flushed. I keep touching her face, telling her to stay awake. I'm freaking out, so I grab my phone to look up side effects of the morning after pills. "Stomach ache, head ache, bleeding, nothing about fucking sounding like a drunk lunatic. What am I gonna do? Marina, you gotta pull it together babe, you gotta be okay?" I yelled at her as if yelling was going to make the situation any better.

Time seemed to be slowing down, as she continued to look worse and worse. She exhaled hard, and started to make a gurgling sound in her throat. "Oh shit, she doesn't look good at all." I say out loud as if someone else was there to hear me. "Marina, MARINA... Stay with me babe. I'm gonna take you somewhere so you can get help." I grab all her things, toss them in the back of her car, throw on a ball cap and rush out the house with her in thrown over my shoulder.

15 minutes later

85

I pulled the car over a block away from the hospital, and turned off the lights, and gather my thoughts as I begin to give her instructions. I wanted to make sure to minimize my involvement with her tonight, as I don't need any of more of her bullshit in my life. "Marina baby? Baby? I need you to focus right now." Her eyes were glossy, and she didn't seem like she was all the way with me. I just needed her to pay attention long enough to walk her drunk, sick ass into the hospital. "You see those lights up the street? That's the hospital babe. I need you to go up there, and tell them you don't feel well okay. I'll call you tomorrow." Her head bobbed back and forth, not really indicating that she understood me. Call her, shit that's right, I'm all in her phone. I took the phone and put it in my pocket until I could figure out what to do with it. This was not how I remotely imagined this night ending, or this relationship. Nevertheless, now I gotta go my own way, and pretend like none of this shit ever happened to me. I open her door, and give her a push and slumps forward before getting out the car and stumbling up the block. I get out and walked the opposite direction of Marina, but turned around and watched just long enough to see her pass out in front of the hospital entrance. A few minutes later I watched as a group of people ran out to scoop her up, and take her inside. I exhaled, pulled out my phone, and requested a ride come pick me up. I couldn't believe my life had resulted in this, but I guess you gotta do what you gotta do when your life is on the line.

2 Days Later…..

"Marina… Marina?" I could hear the nurse calling my name, but I wasn't able to open my eyes. After focusing on the sound of her voice for a few more seconds, I begin to slowly gain consciousness. "Hi there sweetheart. My name is Rose, and I'm one of your nurses. If you can hear me, raise your left hand?" I felt like I was lifting a twenty pound weight strapped to the back of my hand. "Very good sweetheart. Now Marina, I'm sorry to tell you this, but… you lost the baby." Tears began to swell up in my eyes, and so many thoughts flooded my mind. "What happened to me? How did I even end up in here? And why did I deserve to lose my baby?"

-   Life is fragile. There are those who can be trusted to protect it, and then there are those who… Well those who willingly throw it away.-

Chapter 13

Revelations

Pain, pain go away, don't come back any day. You're not welcome, your not my friend. No one needs you in the end.

Luna

"Tonight local police frantically search to find anyone with information regarding how a twenty-four year old pregnant woman, ended up at St. Mary of Grace Hospital on Wednesday night. The young woman seen here, was found passed out in front of the emergency room entrance shortly after nine pm. She is currently being treated for an accidental drug overdose. If you have any information that will lead to an arrest, please call crime stoppers at 1-555-27CRIME. More at eleven. Back to you with the local weather...."

"I must be tripping. I swear that girl looked like. No, it can't be her." I was laying on the couch flipping through the channels, when I stopped on the local news as they were covering a story about a young woman who was drugged and dumped at the hospital. I couldn't say for sure, since they didn't share her name, but I swear the woman they showed on the screen was Marina, the girl I was using to get back at Dev. I picked up my phone, scrolled through my call log, to check and see when was the last time I heard from her. "Monday night? Shit, I better give her a call. Hopefully I'm losing my mind, and she's alright." I click on her name, but instead of ringing, her phone goes straight to voicemail. *"We're sorry, the person you are trying to reach has a mailbox that is full. Please try your call again later."* No matter how many times I call, her voice mail recording played each time. "This isn't happening. I should just go up there and see what is going on. That wouldn't hurt. Just to be safe." Wasting no time, I throw on my shoes and a light jacket, run out of the house, and speed across town towards the hospital. This has to be a bad dream, there is no way she could have ended up in this predicament.

The hospital was so cold and sterile. It had been years since I had been inside of one as a visitor, and never as a patient. I strolled down the halls occasionally peeking into some of the rooms, seeing all the people suffering from various injuries or illnesses, and I begin to feel somewhat responsible for whatever ultimately happened to Marina. She is truly an innocent victim, and whether Dev did this or not, knowing that she was really pregnant, I can only hope that she doesn't blame me for getting her caught up in all this mess.

The ER reception desk was exactly where the woman downstairs told me it would be. Dead center in the middle of the fourth floor to the right of the elevators. I rush over towards the chubby woman sitting behind the counter, who was typing away on a computer, not paying any attention to the multitude of people walking around on the floor. I stand directly in front of her waving my hand quickly attempting to get her attention. I'm panting from the quick sprint over, and after a few seconds I say hello, since she never broke her focus from looking at the screen. "Uhhh. Hi." I say again, but she won't acknowledge me. "Hi, my name is Lu…" She interrupts me. "Patients First and Last name, age, and room number." "Ohh, well Marina Cooper, twenty-four, I don't know her room number." She types feverously and follows up with secondary questions. "Relation to the patient, and are you aware of visiting hours?" I'm beginning to grow impatient with her lack of human decency, and common courtesy; so I snap my fingers in her face. "Look, Ma'am! Bertha, since that's what your tag says. I'm trying to find out why my cousin is laying in a hospital bed, and why I had to see her face on the **seven o'clock** news. Either you can help me, or get me someone else who can." She stopped typing, and slowly looked up from her screen. "Give me your id, take this badge, and her room number is 1572." I apologize for being rude, and thank her over and over again. She rolls her eyes with a gruff, starts to take down information from my driver's license, hands me a badge, and points to her left, indicating her room was in that direction.

As I approach the door, I hear her whimpering quietly over the sound of the oxygen monitor that beeped every few seconds. "Knock, Knock… You feel up to having a visitor?" I ask softly as I peak my head in the door. She wiped her eyes and sat up in the bed. "Hey Luna, how are you doing? You didn't have to come visit me in here. I kinda don't want you to see me like this." Her voice cracked as she attempted to fix herself up, trying to look presentable. Her face was sunken in, and pale. Her hair was pulled into a messy bun on top of her head, and the bags under her eyes were indicative of someone who had been crying non-stop. I walk across the room and take a chair from a table in the corner, and pull it over to sit next to her. "How do you feel? Do you remember what happened? The news said someone dropped you off here? Was it… Did Dev do this?" I ramble off questions without giving her a chance to respond. I didn't want to make a false accusation against Dev, so I was dependent on her to tell me what really happened. For all I know maybe she was into drugs, and he had nothing to do with this at all. Please god, don't let Dev be responsible for this. She took a deep breath and began to explain. "Well I told Dev about the… about my baby. I got pregnant for real Luna. I didn't mean to. Crazy thing is I don't know if it was Dev's baby, or if it was this other guy I slept with. Nonetheless, I wanted to stick to our plan and tell Dev I was pregnant, but I was kinda hoping that he would be excited, and maybe we could have started a real relationship. Although I know he thought I was seventeen. I guess I would have come up with something to tell him regarding why I lied in the first place. I didn't want him to get mad at you." She smiled a little, wiped her nose, and went on. "All I remember is that Dev got really mad when I told him I was pregnant. He flipped out and asked me to get an abortion. Then he texted me later saying that he wanted to talk, and work things out. I went to see him a few days later, cause he made me dinner, and we had a glass of wine. Next thing I know, I'm here, and the nurse told me I lost my baby." She could barely finish her sentence before she burst into tears. My heart instantly broke, and yet I could do nothing. What could he have given her in that drink that caused her to lose her memory, and her baby? No matter the drug, or drugs, he is way more of a monster than I ever imagined. I get up and wrap my arms around her, and just hold her for a moment, trying to calm her down. "I'm really sorry Marina, I wish I could fix this. I should have never got you mixed up with that bastard. Please forgive me." She cried for a few more minutes, until we heard a knock at the door. "Hey, babe how are you…. Luna?" "Terri?" I get up, look at Marina, and quickly back to him. "Terri, what the fuck is going on here?"

Dev

"It had been a couple days since the whole Marina drug incident. I was coming to stay with my mom to get out of Bridgeton. I told my job I had a family emergency, so I would be out for a week. I just wanted to let this thing die down before I went back to my daily life. I must have gotten too comfortable ya know; because clearly I forgot I put the phone, you know Marina's phone, in my overnight bag. That's how you all found me. I'm not going to lie anymore, no need. You know the truth. I gotta own this one. But all of this was an accident. I promise I didn't mean to hurt her." I told the detectives the whole story as I sat in the cold room handcuffed to the table. They both looked at one another, then back to me, and said they'd be right back in a few minutes. The room was oddly similar to the one I sat in when I was a little boy, when I was at the police station snitching on my father. At first when they showed up at my mom's house asking about Marina, I pretended that we both were doing drugs that night, hoping to minimize the fact that she was doped up and abandoned at the hospital alone. That lie lasted about ten minutes since they asked me to take a drug test. Knowing that all they would find in my system was weed, and alcohol, I just came clean and said I would go downtown and talk to them further. They asked me how we knew each other, and how everything ended the night I left her at the hospital. I said I met her on this app, but never mentioned that I knew she was a minor. At first I was told that as long as I plead guilty, I would only be charged with reckless endangerment for accidentally drugging her, then leaving her alone. That was until they found out she was pregnant, and the baby died. Now I'm facing attempted murder, and manslaughter 2. Never thought things would have ended up this way.

That night, after I got home from the hospital, I cleaned the entire house, making sure to wipe everything down, removing any trace of Marina ever being there. As I was finishing up, I called Sherrod to ask him what was in the pills I took from his room. He tells me that as long as I took the off-white ones from the top drawer, then she would have been fine. "Off-white? Bruh I took some bright ass white pills from a zipper bag. What did I give her?" Sherrod flipped out. He claimed they must have been this hybrid drug his boy sold him. Something like a muscle relaxer, hallucinogen, and some other shit. He said he usually only takes half of one. Seeing how I gave her two whole pills, he had no idea what would happen to her. I didn't want to take any chances being caught up in this shit, so I packed a bag, and called my mom saying my house was being fumigated, so I needed to spend a few days with her. Didn't even cross my mind to pitch Marina's phone. So when the police couldn't find it in her purse, or in her car, they used her gps locator to trace its whereabouts, which led them right to me.

Crazy to think that I was so concerned with having gotten some minor pregnant, but come to find out, Marina was just a few years younger than me. Now I feel really stupid for not asking more personal questions. I still don't know why she would lie about her age, or why she didn't just come out and tell me how old she was when she dropped the news that she was pregnant. I probably would have made a different choice. Then again, maybe I wouldn't have trusted her either way. I guess I'll never find out who she really was, or why she lied in the first place, since now I'm facing seven to ten years in the pen. I have nothing but time on my hands to think about what went down.

The detectives come back into the room, read me my charges, hand me a piece of paper asking me to sign my confession, and say someone will be back shortly to take me into custody. If my dad could only see me now, I wonder if he would be proud of the man I've become. Just like him.

Luna

"What is going on Marina? Why is Terri here?" I stood up and calmly walked backwards until I was standing next to the emergency button, which hung on the wall above her bed. I was ready to push it and scream for help, since the last time I saw Terri, I had covered the outside of his car with glitter paint, and covered his interior with pig intestines. So I'm pretty sure I'm not his favorite person right now. Terri puts his hands in the air and side steps into the room keeping his back as close to the other wall as he could. "It's okay Luna, this is that other guy I was telling you about. I thought you and Terri were friends? Is there something I don't know about?" Terri chimed in. "Yeah, you didn't know that this crazy bitch and her friends cost me fifteen thousand dollars in damages to my car. Or that she graciously created multiple social media pages with my name, face, and all my personal information on em' calling me a lying ass cheater." He said to Marina, then turned his attention back to me. "I was put on probation at work because of your little stunts. Why are you here Luna? That's a better question." The rage in Terri's voice was petrifying. I couldn't sit down until I found out how they knew each other. Knowing his lifestyle, I wasn't surprised that she had slept with his nasty ass too. Marina asked us both to calm down, as she started to explain their history. "About three years ago, I met Terri while I was working as an intern at his office. At first it was just a business mentorship thing between us; but over time it became much more. I learned so much about him

93

professionally, that I really admired him. Then to find out that Terri was a polygamist, I thought it was cool that he was so open sexually. We started hanging out after work, and would occasionally mess around, but that was until he started getting serious in a couple of his relationships. I left the internship, because it didn't pay enough, and my dad got really sick and needed help around the house. Terri and I remained friends, and helped me get some part-time work with another company he knew of in the city. Since that job wasn't paying enough to keep me afloat, that's when you and I met; you know when you saw my ad for escort services. I knew Terri wouldn't agree with what I was doing, so I never let him told him about my escort life. Then I found out that you and Terri were friends, because the first night I hooked up with Dev, he saw his picture in my phone, and basically explained that you two were messing around. I never said anything to you either, because I knew it would just be too much to handle." I sat down in the chair and shook my head in disbelief. I had no idea Marina's life was so complex. I guess because I was so busy paying her to help me get back at my ex, that I never thought to talk to her about her life, like a human. Terri slowly walked over to the bed, and hugged Marina for a second, but never took his eyes off of me. I stood up, grabbed my jacket off the chair, and start walking towards the door. Before leaving, I turned back around and offered the most genuine apology I've ever given anyone. I could have gotten this girl killed, all over trying to get revenge on a stupid ex boyfriend. "Marina, I truly apologize for everything I did getting you caught up in this mess. I never wanted to hurt you. I hope you can forgive me one day." She smiled and shook her head with understanding.

As I was walking down the hall, I heard Terri say my name, as he jogged up the hall to catch me. "Luna, wait up. Can we talk?" I stopped in the middle of the floor, and drop my head as I turned around in his direction. "Terri. I have nothing to say. Well, I will say that I'm sorry for what I did to your car. And for the websites. And for the, you know bowel situation." He smiled and laughed softly. "Yeah, I was shitting for hours because of whatever you put in my drink." We both burst into laughter. "No, but really Lu. I'm sorry I never told you the truth. And I'm sorry I hurt you the way I did. If I could do it all over again. I would have kept it 100 from the beginning, and given you the choice of choosing how you wanted to deal with me. Guess selfishness got in the way." "Yeah I guess it did. You know what Terri. I forgive you. Now you go take care of Marina, she's the one who really needs your support right now. But thank you." I lean in and kiss his cheek, and turn to walk away.

Never in a million years would I have imagined that all of this would have transpired, simply from breaking up with one guy. I turned into a woman I never wanted to be, and Dev was truly more screwed up than I ever thought. The painful secrets from my past, I'm sure will haunt me for years to come. One thing's for sure, the Luna I was four months ago, that girl is dead and gone. However, the Luna I am today will never be the same.

www.ingramcontent.com/pod-product-compliance
Lightning Source LLC
Chambersburg PA
CBHW020542130626
46552CB00007B/2725